WHAT'S NEXT?

The *West Wing* Guide to American Democracy

SCOTT ROBINSON

ISBN 979-8655572881

Author photograph by Joshua Robinson

For my dear friend
Laura Walter

Also by Scott Robinson...

<u>What's Next?</u>
The West Wing Guide to American Democracy
The West Wing Guide to Global Politics
The Quotable West Wing:
          The Wit and Wisdom of the Bartlet White House
The West Wing Ultimate Superfan Trivia Challenge!
The West Wing Big Book of Superfan Fun!
By Those Who Show Up:
          The West Wing Guide to Progressive Action

<u>Red Brains, Blue Brains</u>
The Psychology of MAGA
Authoritarian We Will Go!
One Big Happy Family

<u>They Long to End Democracy</u>
The GOP
The Christian Nationalists
The Oligarchy
Minority Rule on the March (omnibus)

<u>Zero-Sum Freedom</u>
The Problem of Freedom
The Nature of Freedom
The Assault on Freedom
The Path to Freedom
The Future of Freedom
Freedom Confounded
Zero-Sum Freedom: Democracy vs. Oligarchy in the Battle for
Liberty (omnibus)

Table of Contents

Introduction

Welcome back to *The West Wing*!

As you're reading this, I can assume several things: 1) you *love* the show! 2) you love the country it's set in; and 3) you're inquisitive, and a thinker. How do I know? I've met dozens of you!

This book, which dives into the broad array of political principles and issues the show presented and maps them to the politics of the real America, before and since the show, took about four years to write. I first went to work when I realized I'd been rewatching the series over and over (via DVD box sets) without even thinking about it. Joining several online *West Wing* groups, I realized others were doing the same thing, and from their comments it became clear that they, as I, had had their political perceptions shaped and their convictions sharpened through this ritual. Many of us had begun observing and questioning the world much as our heroes do.

So I started putting the ideas we saw in *The West Wing* together with what we were seeing in the real world of US politics. That was a particularly telling exercise, during the presidency of Donald Trump.

I don't want the tone or structure of the essays to convey in any way that I suffer from the illusion that I am teaching anybody anything; though I present a lot of historical information and current events, as well as some political theory, I hasten to say that I'm no expert, just a fan who was once a journalist. I'm just sharing what I picked up as I got more and more interested in the things Aaron Sorkin was writing about. And he admits this same thing about himself; he's no political pundit, and he knew next to nothing about politics when he started writing the show. He just shared what he was picking up along the way.

In addition to the themes and issues from the show, I've offered up a context based on ideas the show never really probed – *neoliberalism*, which is the ideology behind what we often called "Reaganomics"; and *authoritarianism*, a word we hear all the time now, based on our current political landscape. These ideas offer a framework within which we can better understand all the themes and issues that *were* in the show. I hope this helps, and appreciate your indulgence.

And I think it's only fair to say, right up front, that what follows is openly partisan. My journalism days are far behind me, and there's nothing at all objective in the text to come. The tone of these essays is openly liberal-progressive. And that's not an apology; I don't have a problem with it, as *The West Wing* itself is openly liberal-progressive. Fair enough?

I very much hope you enjoy your brief stay here, and thank you so much for sharing the grand adventure of *The West Wing* with me!

STR
September 2023

Decisions Are Made by Those Who Show Up

Generational Disaffection in the Political Process

President Bartlet is in a town hall meeting with a large group of young people at the Newseum in Roslynn, Virginia. Most of his staff are with him, behind the scenes, as well as daughter Zoey, who was dragged there by dad. It's been a busy, tense day, with an F-117 pilot missing in the Iraqi No-Fly Zone and Toby's astronaut brother stranded in earth orbit; and it's about to get far worse, as a pair of white supremacist assassins wait outside in hiding.

"Here's an answer to your question that I don't think you're going to like," Bartlet is saying to a young woman in the audience. "The current crop of 18-to-25-year-olds is the most politically apathetic generation in American history. In 1972, half of that age group voted. In the last election, 32%. Your generation is considerably less likely than any previous one to write or call public officials, attend rallies, or work on political campaigns. A man once said this: 'Decisions are made by those who show up.' So are we failing you, or are you failing us? It's a little of both.

"There's a guy on my staff who showed me a report from the Center of Policy Alternatives that said 61% of your age group agree with the statement, 'Politicians and political officials have failed my generation.' When asked how older generations see you, your answers were 'lazy', 'confused', and 'unfocused'; when asked how you see yourselves, your answers were 'ambitious', 'determined', and 'independent'.

"See, all that ambition and determination doesn't translate into political action, Suzanne."

At this writing, more than 20 years have passed since "What Kind of Day Has It Been?"[1] first aired, and Zoey's Generation X is no longer the youngest; the Millennials, born between the mid-Eighties and the Millennium, have grown up, and Gen Z (21st century kids) now hold the title. Zoey is 18 on the occasion above, which puts her at the very end of Gen X and just a little too old for Millennial status.

President Barlet produces some statistics above, and knowing Aaron Sorkin, they were real numbers that were accurate in 2000. What are the Younger Generation numbers today?

Half of all Millennials don't vote, according to Jason Zenor, reporting data in the *Florida Communication Journal*[2] in 2018; a fourth aren't even registered. Of those who are registered to vote, only 50 percent have a political affiliation.

Zenor's paper identifies four factors that explain this disaffection. The first is that partisan media drives the partisan system; Millennials see no objective source of true. The second is their belief that the system cannot be changed. The third is that the broken political system leaves them powerless, and the fourth is that while they do not see our political system as innately evil, they do feel it has been usurped by people who are.

There's irony, of course, in this unfortunate deterioration of faith in government in our young people; they will inherit the US in 25 years, and will hold the power they now see as beyond them. It is surely worse now than it was in Zoey Barlet's college days.

"This is the part where Zoey tries to crawl under a seat to hide," Barlet continues, after pointing Zoey out in the audience. "Don't worry about it, sweetie, I'll bring out the baby pictures any second now."

He proceeds to underscore how taxation is rising as benefits accruing to young Americans are receding:

---

[1] S1E22.

[2] In *Florida Communication Journal*, Spring 2018, Vol. 46, Issue 1, p91-105.

"...that tax burden has crept further and further down the income and age ladder," he says, "and benefits are going more and more to the elderly and well-to-do... We spend nine times as much on the elderly as we do on a single child. No wonder this upcoming generation has turned its back on a government that's forgotten them.

"Overall entitlement payments have crowded out public investment in infrastructure and they will have crowded out public investment in education., to say nothing of the general quality of life. So college kids are facing a future of having to pay higher taxes...

"[According to the] Generation X advocacy group Third Millennium, 53 percent of 18-to-25-year-olds believe the soap opera *General Hospital* will outlast Medicare," Barlet tells the kids. "This from a generation convinced that the generation before them has ransomed their generation's future. That's why my youngest daughter Zoey is always mad at me..."

President Bartlet's summary of the young generation's predicament is sobering: it speaks to a systemic disenfranchisement of those whose stake in the US is ultimately greatest, a damning indictment of those in power today and a none-too-rosy portrait of challenges to come. His typical reliance upon hard numbers and blunt realities don't exactly inspire his audience.

And there's considerable irony in that: as hope for the future has receded, the attributes of the young have, over the quarter century, skewed further and further toward the values that define the American ideal. Put another way, they are more and more the sort of people who are best equipped, moving forward, to realize the America that has always beckoned as the best possible.

Stella Rouse of the University of Maryland and Ashley Ross of Texas A&M summarize those attributes:[3] the persona of the Millennial Generation, they report, is built on these characteristics – diversity (racial and ethnic); tolerance; a hunger for social justice;

---

[3] In *The Politics of Millennials: Political Beliefs and Policy Preferences of America's Most Diverse Generation*, University of Michigan Press, 2018.

common struggle with economic difficulties; cosmopolitan identity, and a poignant disinterest in traditional institutions.

This mix of attributes is a recipe for success as a nation. It captures all that is best and most appropriate in the leaders of tomorrow. Those of us who are older can look at that list and feel a longing to see those traits in our peers. All the more ironic, then, that the generation poised to inherit the country face even greater struggles, when their turn comes.

The picture wasn't so great when Bartlet was painting it, and it has deteriorated considerably in the years since. Even so, he is able to turn things around with a simple truth that accrues to no specific generation, but holds sway across them all, offering the reins back to that disaffected generation.

"They're telling me that we're out of time," Bartlet tells the kids. "I just want to mention that at several points during the evening, I was referred to as both a liberal and a populist. And the fellow fourth from the back called me a socialist. Which was nice, I hadn't heard that for a while.

"Actually, I'm an economics professor. My great-grandfather's great-grandfather was Dr. Josiah Bartlet, who was the New Hampshire delegate to the second Continental Congress, the one that sat in session in Philadelphia in the summer of 1776 and announced to the world that we were no longer subjects of King George III, but rather a self-governing people. We hold these truths to be self-evident, they said. That all men are created equal. Strange as it may seem, that was the first time in history that anyone had ever bothered to write that down. Decisions are made by those who show up. Class dismissed."

Decisions are made by those who show up. It's one of the simplest, most straightforward chestnuts Bartlet ever uttered – but it's the best, most righteous answer to our children's disillusionment.

"One last thing: while you may be mistaking this for your monthly meeting of the Ignorant Tight-Ass Club, in this building, when the President stands, *nobody* sits."

~President Bartlet

"I like to show off..."

The Perils of Classified Information

Someone in the Bartlet White House is leaking classified information.

Two bits of information tip off the new associate counsel, Joe Quincy: a question from a White House press corps science reporter asking if the White House is suppressing evidence of life on Mars, and another reporter asking CJ's office if the White House bargained with the Justice Department to call off an anti-trust investigation.[4]

Quincy talks to Josh, and the two of them go to Leo:

"Mr. McGarry, the press secretary came to me with a question from the *Post*'s science editor, who has a source claiming that a NASA study was classified at the urging of the White House," Quincy says.

"What do they think it said?"

"They claim it said that a meteorite from Mars... was discovered about thirty years ago and that we found carbonate molecules. That we know there's life on Mars. That's what they're saying we're suppressing."

"The Defense Department classified the NASA Commission report," Leo says.

"The report exists?"

"Well, I can't tell you that, Joe, the report was classified. But I can tell you that it was classified by the Defense Department."

While everybody absorbs that one, Josh speaks up:

"Did we get the Justice Department to call of its anti-trust investigation with Casseon?"

"They didn't call it off. They settled."

Josh turns to Donna. "Tell him what the *Post* said we got in exchange for calling off Justice."

"One hundred thousand computers in classrooms."

---

[4] In "Life on Mars", S4E21.

Leo, surprised, nods. "That was part of the settlement – one hundred thousand computers."

"There's a leak," Josh concludes. "This, Mars... who knew about the terms with Casseon outside of us?"

"The President, me and you, Counsel, Counsel at Treasury and Commerce. Two, three guys at NEC," Leo replies. "Hackley, Little, May..."

"The Vice President," Josh adds.

Later, Quincy does some digging and connects Vice President Hoynes to the gossip columnist at the *Post*, who writes about a book deal by a Washington socialite Hoynes has been calling frequently from White House telephones.

"Mr. Vice President, have you been having an affair with Helen Baldwin while here at the White House?" Josh asks Hoynes directly when he, Quincy, Toby and CJ go to his office that evening to confront him.

Toby begins to explain. "He's asking because-"

"I know why he's asking," Hoynes replies. "I like to show off... I said things. I said I'd seen proof of life on Mars. I'd said I intervened at the Justice Department to put one hundred thousand computers into classrooms. I thought it made me sound like a good guy."

Finally, Hoynes stands before the president and Leo on the walkway outside the Oval Office:

"I'm resigning the Vice Presidency," he declares.

"What about 'It's none of your business?'" Bartlet asks.

"I leaked classified information," Hoynes replies. "It *is* their business. It's also a felony."

When the existence of a secret US space shuttle, a military shuttle, is made public by Greg Brock of the *New York Times*, the West Wing goes on high alert, as this represents an egregious security breach – public disclosure of incredibly sensitive, highly classified information. Brock goes to jail, as he will not reveal his source.

A hunt for the leaker ensues, with White House Counsel Oliver Babish leading the charge. He focuses on CJ, now the new White House chief of staff, as the most likely suspect. When it becomes clear that the quest to pin down the leaker may lead to a subpoena issued to Leo McGarry, who is on the campaign trail with Matt Santos as the potential next vice president, Toby steps forward and confesses to CJ that it was he who leaked the information about the shuttle. He is immediately fired by the president and escorted from the White House, ending his tenure as White House communications director.[5]

When we first saw these events in *The West Wing*'s 4th and 6th seasons years ago, they both seemed gravely serious. And, of course, both ended up creating unprecedented crises.

Today, however, Hoynes' crimes and Toby's disclosure – bragging about having seen a nerdy NASA report and whispering about Justice Department settlements, trying to save the lives of three astronauts – seem downright quaint. Because here in the 2020s, the mishandling of classified information has taken on a whole new look and feel. A whole new *intensity*.

At this writing, former president Donald Trump stands accused of stealing classified documents (including Department of Defense military plans, and even nuclear profiles of other nations), denying having them, refusing to return them, and conspiring with staff at his Mar-a-Lago retreat to destroy evidence that they had made efforts to hide them.

Donald Trump, like John Hoynes, likes to show off.

The former president has, post-Oval, become history's poster child for the mishandling of classified information. He was indicted in June of 2023, charged with 32 counts of willfully retaining classified documents pertaining to national defense after leaving office, and an additional 8 counts (as of July), which include making false statements and engaging in a conspiracy to obstruct justice. It was the first-ever federal indictment of an ex-president. These are criminal charges under the Espionage Act.

The entire world knows, of course, what this is about: the former president accumulated many boxes of documents (including the

---

[5] The story is an arc across several episodes. Toby departs in "Here Today", S7E5.

classified ones) at his Mar-a-Lago estate in Florida, and when asked to return them by the National Archives and Records Administration, proceeded to

- Deny that he had them
- Claim they belonged to him
- Return a few but keep others
- Declare that he had telepathically de-classified them
- Hide the ones he hadn't turned over
- Instruct his Mar-a-Lago staff to shell-game them in bathrooms and storerooms
- Attempt to destroy evidence that he'd done so

Most anyone who watches television or social media has seen all this play out, and knows that the classified documents Trump took and tried to hang onto included information concerning national defense, the weapons capabilities of the US (and other countries), US nuclear programs, military vulnerabilities of the US and its allies, and military retaliation plans.

The sources of the documents, 102 in all, include the CIA, the NSA, the DoD, the National Geospatial Intelligence Agency, the Department of Energy, the Department of State and its Bureau of Intelligence Research, and the National Reconnaissance Office, according to the indictment.

It also says that some of the classified information included "could put at risk the national security of the United States, foreign relations, the safety of the United States military and human sources, and the continued viability of sensitive intelligence collection methods."

Most jaw-dropping of all is an audio tape obtained from CNN by Jack Smith, the special prosecutor appointed to investigate the issue, of Trump in his Bedminster, New Jersey digs with staffers and writers, acknowledging both his possession of the documents and his understanding that he no longer had the authority to de-classify anything. In the process, he presents those assembled with a classified Pentagon document about a potential plan to attack Iran:

TRUMP: "He said that I wanted to attack Iran, Isn't it amazing? I have a big pile of papers, this thing just came up. Look. This was him. They presented me this – this is off the record but – they presented me this. This was him. This was the Defense Department and him."

TRUMP: "I was just thinking, because we were talking about it. And you know, he said, 'He wanted to attack Iran, and what...These are the papers." [He presents the Iran attack plan.] "This was done by the military and given to me..." [He then mentions that the plan is classified.) "See as president I could have declassified it. Now I can't, you know, but this is still a secret."

STAFFER: "Now we have a problem."

TRUMP: "Isn't that interesting? It's so cool. I mean, it's so, look, her and I, and you probably almost didn't believe me, but now you believe me."

WRITER: "No, I believed you."

TRUMP: "It's incredible, right?"

WRITER: "No, they never met a war they didn't want."

TRUMP: "Hey, bring some, uh, bring some Cokes in, please."

At this writing, the trial is set for May 20, 2024.

Trump isn't the only president to get careless with classified information. According to William Bosanko, chief operating officer of the National Archives, "I will tell you this: every PRA administration from Reagan forward, we have found classified information in unclassified boxes."

Nor is this carelessness confined to the Oval Office. There were 98 classified documents in the papers of Sen. Edmund Muskie, ME-D, that he had turned over to the library at Bates College. "Since about 2010, we have gotten over 80 calls from different libraries where mostly Members of Congress have taken papers and deposited them in libraries for collections, their own papers," according to Mark Bradley of the Information Security Oversight Office.

And it's not just an issue of carelessness. There's the case of the Valerie Plame incident during the Bush II Administration, in which Plame – a covert CIA operative – was publicly outed as an act of political retribution.

In 2002, Plame had written a CIA-internal memo expressing uncertainty about her husband Joseph Wilson, a former diplomat, undertaking a mission to Niger to investigate whether or not Iraq had attempted to purchase uranium there. She granted that Wilson might be of some use. When President Bush said, in 2003, that Saddam Hussein had tried to purchase uranium in Africa – which had not been established as fact – Wilson wrote an op-ed in the *New York Times*, publicly expressing doubt that any such purchase had been made.

A week later, an article by journalist Robert Novak in *The Washington Post* exposed that Plame worked for the CIA and that she had recommended Wilson for the Niger investigation. Plame's covert CIA role was classified information, leaked to Novak by Karl Rove and Scooter Libby (of Bush's administration) and Richard Armitage of the State Department. A grand jury investigation followed, as well as Congressional investigations, and Scooter Libby was convicted of lying to investigators.[6]

These real-world instances of mishandling of classified information cover the same spread we've seen in *The West Wing*. There's the showing-off, making oneself seem like a big deal because of what they know (Hoynes and Trump); there's risk to national security (Toby revealing the existence of a military space shuttle, with all the destabilizing international implications; Trump casually handing out invasion plans to writers).

We also must acknowledge that sometimes these things are inadvertent: Edmund Muskie must not have realized there were

---

[6] Bush commuted his prison sentence; Trump eventually pardoned him.

classified documents in his papers, because he's a smart man, and would have realized that turning them over to a college library was just asking for trouble. (In that same vein, we can understand that Joe Biden, Mike Pence, and Hillary Clinton were unaware that there was classified information in their parlor; there would be no gain for any of them, and only trouble if they didn't promptly turn it in.)

We can admire Sorkin and the latter-day *West Wing* writers for treating this subject with the seriousness they did, in an era when the true gravity of it wasn't yet as up in our faces as it is today. There's real risk happening here: the covers of covert operatives can be blown, endangering their lives; hostile foreign powers can be tipped off to US weaknesses they can exploit; relations between the US and its allies can be compromised by their realization that their secrets might not be so safe in our hands.

And even though Richard Schiff hated what the writers had Toby doing at the time, *The West Wing* surges past the real world, once again, in its dramatization of a critical issue: Toby's leak of the military shuttle's existence may have compromised national security and the Bartlet Administration's standing with other nations, but it was a matter of moral trade-off. He did what he did for the noblest of purposes, to save the lives of three stranded astronauts. We love Toby and *The West Wing* precisely because they act from such a serious, honorable place.

"Say they are smug and superior. Say their approach to public policy makes you want to tear your hair out. Say they like high taxes and spending your money. Say they want to take your guns and open your borders, but don't call them worthless. At least don't do it in front of me. The people I have met have been extraordinarily qualified. Their intent is good. Their commitment is true. They are righteous, and they are patriots. And I'm their lawyer."

~Ainsley Hayes

"In a country born on a will to be free, what could be more fundamental than this?"

The Right of Privacy

Supreme Court Justice Crouch is retiring, giving President Bartlet an opportunity to name a new Supreme Court justice. The staff has vetted Peyton Cabot Harrison III, an accomplished jurist of great repute. Toby, Josh and Sam are all confident of a certain and speedy confirmation.[7]

But an anonymous tipster makes Sam aware that Harrison holds the belief that the US Constitution does not guarantee American citizens the right to privacy. This is highly controversial, and deeply disturbs Sam, who reads a paper written by Harrison late in his law school days, confirming the position. He immediately urges the others to reconsider recommending that the president nominate Harrison for the seat.

Harrison comes in for an Oval Office chat. Bartlet, Toby and Sam all ask Harrison a series of questions, then confront him directly on the paper he wrote 30 years earlier. Harrison candidly admits he does not believe the Constitution confers a right to privacy:

"Judges are bound to interpret the Constitution within the strict parameters of the text itself," Harrison says, "The Constitution doesn't provide for a right of privacy. The right doesn't exist."

"The third amendment says soldiers can't be quartered in private homes," Sam replies. "The fifth provides protection against self-incrimination, and the fourth against unreasonable searches. You deny the right to privacy lived in those passages?"

---

[7] In "The Short List", S1E9.

"No. I do not deny it, but the fact that the Framers enumerated those specific protections is all the more reason to believe that they had no intention of making privacy a *de facto* right."

"They'd just fought a revolution; they had no question of their freedoms. The Bill of Rights was meant to codify the most crucial of those rights, not to limit the others.

"In 1787, there was a sizable block of delegates who were initially opposed to the Bill of Rights. One member of the Georgia delegation had this to say by way of opposition: 'If we list this set of rights, some fools in the future are going to claim that people are entitled only to those rights enumerated and no longer.' The Framers knew-"

"Were you just calling me a fool, Mr. Seaborn?"

"I wasn't calling you a fool, sir, the brand-new state of Georgia was."

"Gentlemen, laws must emanate from the Constitution."

"There are natural laws, judge."

"I do not deny there are natural laws, Mr. Ziegler. I only deny that judges are empowered to enforce them."

"Then who will?"

After Harrison leaves the Oval, Sam speaks up.

"It's about the next 20 years," Sam argues. "In the Twenties and Thirties, it was the role of government. Fifties and Sixties, it was civil rights. The next two decades, it's gonna be *privacy*. I'm talking about the Internet. I'm talking about cellphones. I'm talking about health records, and who's gay and who's not.

"And moreover, in a country born on a will to be free, what could be more fundamental than this?"

Sam was spot-on there. In the 20 years since that episode aired, social media has arrived; cell phones became smart phones, by which text messages and emails could be accessed; the cloud (server farms available to all) became a thing. There's far more personal data than there used to be, and far more ways to get to it.

First, some of the scary side; in recent years, hackers have achieved the following:

- A 2021 cyberattack on Microsoft's Exchange email servers resulted in the theft of the records of 30,000 US companies (twice that many world-wide), rendering their own email servers vulnerable;
- A series of attacks on Yahoo by Russian hackers resulted in the exposure of 3 billion user accounts;
- 530 million Facebook user accounts were exposed in 2021, and data from this hack was later found sitting in public Amazon S3 cloud servers;
- Facebook's woes had already begun years earlier, when the British firm Cambridge Analytica stole almost 100 million Facebook user accounts and then sold them; Facebook did nothing to stop them. It took an unprecedented $5 billion fine by the Federal Trade Commission to move Facebook to action;
- In 2019, 885 million records were leaked from First American Financial Corp., including bank account numbers, bank statements, wire transfer receipts, and drivers' license numbers;
- In 2014, 76 million families and 7 million businesses were compromised when their accounts at JPMorgan Chase were accessed through a Russion cyberattack.

So the world is scarier now than when Sam made his prediction. What's in place, legally, to protect us?

Quite a bit, actually. It began with the Privacy Act of 1974, which established a code of "fair information practices" to guard against unwarranted privacy invasions. More specific law followed, such as the well-known Health Insurance Portability and Accountability Act (HIPAA) of 1996, which protects personal health information – especially important in an era when that information has to move around digitally, and between many different parties.

The Electronic Communications Privacy Act protects electronic communications of all kinds against unauthorized access, use, and disclosure; the Computer Fraud & Abuse Act makes illegal the unauthorized access of computers and other digital devices, as well as activities pursuant to such access (harvesting and traffic of passwords, for instance); the Financial Services Modernization Act regulates personal information collected by financial institutions, requiring those institutions to issue customer notifications regarding use of their data; the Fair and Accurate Credit Transactions Act requires financial institutions to implement identity theft protection.

And the good old Federal Communications Commission protects "customer proprietary network information" held by Internet service providers and other digital communications carriers (the locations of mobile devices; phone numbers used by a consumer; metadata for each call, etc.). The Telecommunications Act requires the provider/carrier to provide such information only 1) as required by law; 2) with the customer's approval; 3) to locate the customer in the event of a 911 call.

And in the era of the cloud, public digital storage providers have entered the fray. For instance, laws are in place today to compel those providers to keep customer data secure. If your phone/text messages are synced to Apple's iCloud, Apple can only be forced to turn it over in response to a warrant associated with a criminal procedure (so think long and hard before you sync your mobile devices to clouds).

So it seems Sam was right: this *is* the age of privacy, and it's driven by cell phones and the Internet, as he predicted. It's scarier now than it was then, but not so much because of justices on benches; it's more a matter of escalating technological progress, our rapidly-expanding use of the Internet, and increasing tech proficiency among bad actors/nations. But we've stayed awake, and the law is keeping up. We just need to be certain we stay awake, and don't fall behind.

"I just want to mention that at several points during the evening, I was referred to as both a liberal and a populist. And the fellow fourth from the back called me a socialist. Which was nice, I hadn't heard that for a while. Actually, I'm an economics professor. My great-grandfather's great-grandfather was Dr. Josiah Bartlet, who was the New Hampshire delegate to the second Continental Congress, the one that sat in session in Philadelphia in the summer of 1776 and announced to the world that we were no longer subjects of King George III, but rather a self-governing people. We hold these truths to be self-evident, they said. That all men are created equal. Strange as it may seem, that was the first time in history that anyone had ever bothered to write that down. Decisions are made by those who show up."

~President Bartlet

"You will be held responsible for shutting down the federal government."

Political Brinkmanship

In the wake of Hoynes' resignation and President's Bartlet's temporary ceding of his authority to Speaker Walken, a new Republican Speaker – Jeff Haffley – now speaks for the House in its negotiations with the White House over the federal budget. And he's not shy about exploiting the leverage he possesses.[8]

"I'm sorry I couldn't give more notice," he tells the president in the Roosevelt Room, "but I just came from our conference, and I had significant opposition to only one percent." (The White House had agreed to one-percent budget cuts across the board.)

"We had a deal at one percent," President Bartlet reminds him.

"But now my members have to go back to their districts for the holidays, explain why we kept the gravy train running with a rising deficit and an economy crying out for tax relief. It's an economic situation that calls for action, not status quo spending. Now three percent may sound painful but it's only for two months. It'll show we're serious."

"What's next? In two months. Five percent? Fifty? How many rounds do we go, Jeff?"

"There is no 'next', sir. I mean not to get too technical, but this government runs out of money at midnight. And my guys are going home. This is it."

Bartlet thinks about it, then shakes his head.

"No."

He stands to leave.

"There is no altering this offer, Mr. President," Haffley says.

---

[8] In "Separation of Powers", S5E7.

"And I said no."

"Let's be clear, sir. We cannot, we will not, vote to keep on footing the bill. You will be held responsible for shutting down the federal government."

"Then shut it down."

And he leaves.

Haffley is practicing *brinkmanship* – trying to win a confrontation or gain an advantage over an opponent by pushing events to a dangerous point of engagement. It's another way of saying 'playing chicken', seeing who will blink first – but with very risky consequences. It's the deliberate escalation of threats to hasten the achievement of one's goals.

Brinkmanship has been both a political and military technique for countless centuries, and can be unfortunately all too effective. Here in the modern era, when we fancy ourselves enlightened, we might have hoped there was no longer a need for such a crude and perilous tool in the hands of our leaders – but there it is.

And all of these brinkmen (and brinkwomen) are, like Haffley, spouting pure bullshit. In the case of the latter, Haffley's budget showdown with President Bartlet had nothing to do with his justifying claims – turning off the "gravy train" in the face of a rising deficit.

Nope. Congressional Republicans (and presidents, for that matter) love to go on about deficits and the federal debt when the Democrats hold power, but when they themselves take power, they spend like drunken sailors (to quote Evelyn Baker Lang). CJ said it best:[9] In *The West Wing* universe, "The Republican Congress spent us into a bottomless hole," just as they do in the real one.

Perhaps the clearest (and most notorious) example of political brinkmanship is the 1962 Cuban Missile Crisis, the 13-day conflict between the US and Soviet Union over the deployment of nuclear weapons in Cuba, 90 miles off the Florida coast. Eschewing knee-jerk military solutions (to his credit), President Kennedy nonetheless

---

[9] In "Institutional Memory", S7E21.

took his Red Rover, Red Rover diplomacy right to the edge, establishing a blockade around Cuba and daring the Soviet navy to breach it. Deploying the missiles in the first place was an act of brinkmanship on the part of Premier Khrushchev, certainly, daring Kennedy to do something about it. Their two-week dance came within hours of breaking down into nuclear confrontation, or the outbreak of conventional war in Berlin, at the very least.

Speaker Haffley's somewhat less cataclysmic brinkmanship, of course, ended up playing out almost note-for-note in the real world a decade after we saw it on the show, as newbie Senator Ted Cruz of Texas took point on a Republican effort to defund the Affordable Care Act – at the time, a law that had been passed but not yet implemented – in exchange for raising the debt ceiling.

Republican lawmakers had agreed amongst themselves in January of 2013 that they would not resort to such tactics, but at summer's end a group of 80 of them nonetheless wrote a letter to then-Speaker John Boehner, urging him to de-fund Obamacare as a condition of any continuing resolution. They then drafted legislation that would strip funding from the ACA while keeping the government open into December.

President Obama made clear he'd veto it, and Cruz grandstanded for 21 hours on the Senate floor, railing against Obamacare – drawing the national spotlight squarely onto himself, and chaining public attention to the showdown for weeks to come.

Boehner moved heaven and earth to force the president to negotiate, and Harry Reid – majority leader of the Democrat-controlled Senate – got into it, stripping the defunding language out of the House legislation.

On October 1, the federal government shut down, and Boehner requested negotiations with the Senate, returning to the original end-Obamacare rhetoric. To save face, he and his caucus began generating piecemeal legislation to continue funding of individual essential programs, which the Senate rejected, insisting that the entire government be reopened. At one point, Boehner blurted out in a press conference that "This isn't some damn game!" - which, of course, it absolutely was, and a game instigated entirely by his 80 members and the preening Cruz.

In his own comments to the press, Obama kept the shutdown squarely on Boehner's shoulders. As the Senate and White House continued not blinking, Boehner began suggesting conciliatory stop-gap measures, as Harry Reid and Mitch McConnell – then the Senate Minority Leader – began working out a deal. On October 16, the date the Cuban Missile Crisis had begun 51 years earlier, the shutdown crisis ended with the announcement of the Reid-McConnell deal, which reopened the government without shutting down Obamacare.

The American public didn't think much of Republican brinkmanship at the time, yet a decade later they made clear they hadn't learned their lesson.

As retribution for the dual impeachments of Donald Trump, the Republican House's extremist wing began demanding the impeachment of President Joe Biden, on the grounds that his son Hunter was clearly a criminal and that he had personally profited from his son's misdeed. Not a shred of evidence was brought forth to support these insinuations, but Georgia Representative Majorie Taylor Greene became the Ted Cruz of the moment, even so, declaring that she would not vote in favor of pending funding legislation unless Speaker Kevin McCarthy, beholden to her for his ascension to the speakership, instituted impeachment proceedings.

Right back where we'd been 10 years earlier, we had to live through yet another take-it-to-the-limit showdown between extreme Republicans holding the nation hostage to get their own way and a White House intent on implementing progressive policy, with a weak House Speaker in the middle.

The West Wing showed us how such confrontations play out. President Bartlet, of course, didn't cave, but was conciliatory to the point of willingness to meet with the Republicans and talk. In the end, he prevailed.

So must it ever be. Brinkmanship, especially in the handling of public policy, is a toxin that must be extricated from our discourse whenever and wherever it surfaces. It is the pinnacle of political irresponsibility, and capitulation to those who would wield it as a weapon must be relentlessly eschewed. To submit to such threats is to open the floodgates to more of the same.

President Bartlet had the right idea.

"We've agreed to call it 'tax relief'..."

The Power of Framing in Political Rhetoric

The new year has arrived, and as Congress reconvenes, a leadership breakfast is being coordinated that will "trumpet a new spirit of bi-partisanship cooperation and understanding in a new year."[10]

Ann Stark, chief of staff to the Republican House Majority Leader, has worked with Toby to negotiate an agreed-upon list of topics to be discussed at the event. The list is presented to the rest of the staff.

"I see we won't be talking about the 993 tax cut," Josh notes.

"We won't be," Leo confirms, "but we've agreed to call it 'tax relief' instead of a tax cut."

"We're calling it 'tax relief'."

"Yeah."

"But we won't be talking about it."

"No."

Josh moves on down the list.

"Leo, the Patient's Bill of Rights-"

"-which we'll be referring to as the Comprehensive Access and Responsibility Act."

Sam is confused.

"What's the Comprehensive Access and Responsibility Act?"

"It's the Patient's Bill of Rights, but the CARA was introduced in 1999. It's fundamentally the same thing and the Republicans have agreed to discuss changing the name back."

"In exchange for calling tax breaks 'tax relief'..."

"-or 'income enhancement'."

---

[10] In "The Leadership Breakfast", S2E11.

Ann Stark knows what she's doing. She's setting up a win for Congressional Republicans that neither the Bartlet team nor the Congressional Democrats even see coming.

"Mr. President, if you read item four you'll see that time at this breakfast will be spent discussing calling the Patient's Bill of Rights the 'Comprehensive Access and Responsibility Act'," Toby later reports in the Oval Office.

"I don't give a damn if they call it the Monroe doctrine!" Bartlet responds. "What the hell are we doing serving Vermont maple syrup?"

Sorkin is being funny with this exchange, of course, but the fact that Ann Stark has negotiated these name changes – and the unfortunate dismissal of those changes by the White House staff – speaks to a very real phenomenon in modern politics.

Metaphors We Live By

George Lakoff, Berkeley cognitive scientist/linguistics expert, is the author of *Metaphors We Live By*, which suggests that we build our internal models of the world out of *frames* driven by concepts about reality that we've absorbed, and expand our understanding by assigning meaning sitting in one frame to the new frames we build.

Put another way, when I hear or experience something new, I will subconsciously push toward an understanding of it by dropping it into a frame I already possess.

Example:

Argument is war

This metaphor takes the concept of *argument* and drops it into the *war* frame I possess. If I take this metaphor on board, then I will assign the features of *war* to my understanding of *argument*: war is *conflict*; there is *a winner and a loser*; the idea is *to defeat the other person*. Argument, in this metaphor, becomes *conflict*, and the objective is to defeat the other.

Then again:

Argument is dance

This metaphor works the same way, but in assigning a different frame, it imbues *argument* with different features: when two people dance, there is *move and countermove*; there is *cooperation*; there is *synchronization*, in varying degrees; and there is *a shared goal*. Viewed within the *dance* frame, *argument* becomes altogether different.

Lakoff isn't just a language expert; he's also a political activist, authoring *The Political Mind* and *Don't Think of an Elephant!*, two books that bring this framing concept into the realm of politics, where it is leveraged to high heaven. Political rhetoric oozes framing language, and it is used to steer our thinking without our realizing it.

Example, from Lakoff:

"Take 'tax relief', a phrase used by the current White House [Bush II]. The word *relief* evokes a conceptual frame of some affliction - an afflicted party, and a reliever who performs the action of relieving. So taxes are an affliction, a reliever is a hero, and anyone who wants to stop him from the relief is a villain. You have just two words, yet all of that is embedded. If you oppose reducing taxes and you use that phrase - *tax relief* - you've already lost."

Put another way,

"For there to be relief, there must be an affliction, an afflicted party, and a reliever who removes the affliction and is therefore a hero. And if people try to stop the hero, those people are villains for trying to prevent relief. When the word tax is added to relief, the result is a metaphor: Taxation is an affliction. And the person who takes it away is a hero, and anyone who tries to stop him is a bad guy. This is a frame. It is made up of ideas, like affliction and hero."

And, as we see above, that's exactly what the Republicans pulled on Toby in negotiating the leadership breakfast.

And here's another Lakoff example quoting Bush II:

Another example Lakoff mentions in his book is when Bush proclaimed in his State of the Union address in January 2005 that "we do not need a permission slip to defend America." Consider what Bush is saying here. Sure, he could have said, "we won't ask permission," but saying "permission slip" evokes the adult-child metaphor, which aligns with conservatives' strict father worldview, according to Lakoff.

The Republicans weren't always so savvy about framing. Lakoff is fond of pointing out that when Nixon got on television and stated, "I am not a crook!", he was foolishly invoking a frame that doomed him: now Americans could see him as nothing *but* a crook.

> "Framing is not primarily about politics or political messaging or communication. It is far more fundamental than that: frames are the mental structures that allow human beings to understand reality – and sometimes to create what we take to be reality. But frames do have an enormous bearing on politics… they structure our ideas and concepts, they shape the way we reason… For the most part, our use of frames is unconscious and automatic." ~Lakoff

The Family-as-Nation Metaphor

Lakoff shares two models that make these behaviors clear. Both are based on the *Family-as-Nation* metaphor – thinking of your country as one big family, and its leaders as your parents. How you then think about your nation depends on your family frame – and Lakoff argues that conservative politicians have mastered the manipulation of that frame.

The Strict Father

"About 35 percent of Americans have what I call 'Strict Father morality'," Lakoff said in an interview on the *Make Me Smart* podcast. "That is, they believe that "father knows best," that father is the authority, that what he says is right, that if children don't obey him, they have to be given tough love and punished until they do – and that this gives rise to a view that you have to be disciplined."

Within this frame, parental authority is just that – authoritarian. The edict of the father is all, and forms the basis of acquiescence to one's social group, one's sociopolitical bias, and in the case of patriarchal religion, one's role in spiritual community.

In his book *Don't Think of an Elephant!*, which is a primer on the framing of political rhetoric, Lakoff points to Evangelical icon James Dobson, of "Focus on the Family" fame, who advocates a particularly harsh agenda for the parenting of very small children, as an example of Strict Father morality and how it works. Human beings are born selfish, in this frame, and must have cooperation and obedience instilled in them through perpetual physical discipline. Lakoff's point is that this mindset remains, long after early childhood has passed.

The Strict Father frame then becomes all-pervasive in the minds of its adherents, Lakoff said, generating a universal hierarchy.

"You have God above Man - we've conquered nature, you have Man above Nature, we can take anything we want for our use – you have the strong

above the weak – that hierarchy follows, from one idea… it's Strict Father Morality applied to all aspects of life."

And this explains Donald Trump, whose victory in 2016 was inexplicable – but no so much as the unwavering support from his conservative, Evangelical base, who continued to support him despite his complete lack of conservative bona fides and his clear commitment to hedonism.

"[Strict Father morality] is what Trump not only believes, but acts on and assumes is correct – and he knows that about 35 percent of the country, the 35 percent who still support him also believe this, even if they're poor. The main thing is, if that is your worldview, and that's your morality, that defines who you are as a person; it's self-definition. And people don't vote against their self-definition. Not only that, it doesn't matter if Trump lies to them, and they know he's lying, because there's a higher truth – which is Strict Father Morality *itself*, which has consequences, and they are truer than any lies – and that if you deny that, if you accept the lies as more important, you're denying your self-identity. That's why there are 'alternative facts'."

The Nurturant Parent

Strict Father Morality is not the end of the story, per Lakoff: There is another parenting style at the other end of the frame, where Mom and Dad are equals, and the upbringing of a child is more a matter of nurture and encouragement than correction and discipline. And this frame also forms the basis of sociopolitical bias and adult moral impetus.

"[This] is what I call 'nurturant morality'," Lakoff said. "That is, you care about other people. In the family, adults care about their children, are honest with them, they try to talk directly with them and have an answer to all their questions, they take care of them and they want them to be fulfilled in life, and they want them to care about other people. And that comes out as a progressive moral view, which goes like this: that citizens care about other citizens, work through the government to provide public resources for everybody, starting with business – you can't have a business if you don't have streets and roads and airports and sewers and science…and that isn't the government, it's the people, the public - the private depends on the public. If you have Strict Father Morality, then you did it all, it's personal responsibility."

Lakoff's ultimate point is devastatingly clear: the Strict Father frame and the Nurturant Parent frame define the politics of our time – and historically, all times – and explain our political and social divides perfectly, while also lending insight into the underlying psychology of our personal worldviews.

Lakoff extends his ideas by pointing out that all voters have at least an innate understanding of both frames, if committing to only one, and that both frames may be activated by language – and this explains the relative success or failure of political rhetoric around us. Greater balance may be achieved in our political discourse, he argues, if all voters can become more aware of political frames and more critical of the rhetoric.

Finally, Lakoff's Strict Father/Nurturant Parent model syncs up nicely with Altemeyer's model of Authoritarianism and the cognitive types of sociopolitical bias: leader-vs-group, threat-vs-opportunity, change-vs-not. It infuses our understanding of irreconcilable worldviews and divisive rhetoric with a renewed sense of possibilities and high utility.

Newt Gingrich uses his words

In the years since, Republicans have come to understand framing thoroughly; they not only actively practice it incessantly (and have for decades), but write playbooks about it.

Newt Gingrich, for instance, when planning his conservative resurgence in Congress in the early Nineties, he wrote a memo that was distributed to Republican officeholders entitled "Language: A Key Mechanism of Control".

"In it, he carried on from Joseph Goebbels, who had repeatedly asserted that in order to control a society, one must first take control of that society's language. Gingrich gave Republicans a list of words to describe anything having to do with Democrats," wrote Thom Hartmann in *The Hidden History of American Oligarchy*:

> *decay, failure (fail), collapse(ing), deeper, crisis, urgent(cy), destructive, destroy, sick, pathetic, lie, liberal, they/them, unionized bureaucracy, "compassion" is not enough, betray, consequences, limit(s), shallow, traitors, sensationalists, endanger, coercion, hypocrisy, radical, threaten, devour, waste, corruption, incompetent, permissive attitude, destructive, impose, self-serving, greed, ideological, insecure, anti-(issue): flag, family, child, jobs; pessimistic, excuses, intolerant, stagnation, welfare, corrupt, selfish, insensitive, status quo, mandate(s) taxes, spend (ing) shame, disgrace, punish (poor . . .), bizarre, cynicism, cheat, steal, abuse of power, machine, bosses, obsolete, criminal rights, red tape, patronage.*

"Gingrich told Republicans that it was as important to characterize themselves in a positive light as it was to trash-talk Democrats. His list of words to apply to themselves and their policies was as follows," Hartmann continued:

share, change, opportunity, legacy, challenge, control, truth, moral, courage, reform, prosperity, crusade, movement, children, family, debate, compete, active(ly), we/us/our, candid(ly), humane, pristine, provide, liberty, commitment, principle(d), unique, duty, precious, premise, care(ing), tough, listen, learn, help, lead, vision, success, empower(ment), citizen, activist, mobilize, conflict, light, dream, freedom, peace, rights, pioneer, proud/pride, building, preserve, pro-(issue): flag, children, environment; reform, workfare, eliminate good-time in prison, strength, choice/choose, fair, protect, confident, incentive, hard work, initiative, common sense, passionate.

"When tyranny begins to emerge, shifts in language become obvious, and it's important to pay close attention to how language is used, especially when certain phrases or memes are used repeatedly," Hartmann wrote. "Tyrants understand that it's more important to control the news than to control the army; armies will follow what they believe to be true, but only when first convinced of its truth, and that requires control of or substantial influence over the news."

So blatant is this usage that it is now a standard practice among Republican lawmakers to simply name things the opposite of what they really are, in order to have them accepted: The Clear Skies Initiative. No Child Left Behind.

Both Lakoff and Hartmann have spent years trying to get Democratic leaders to take this message seriously and to realize that they are only hurting themselves by submitting to the framing used by their opponents, rather than developing their own.

Bill Clinton was the exception, Lakoff noted: he understood framing and how to make it work, not just for him, but against his opposition.

"He stole the other side's language," Lakoff wrote. "He walked about 'welfare reform', for example. He said, 'The age of big government is over.' He did what he wanted to do, only he took their language and used their words to describe it. It made them very mad."

Overtures to both the Obama team and Hillary Clinton team were dismissed, Lakoff has lamented. Either the psychology itself wasn't being taken seriously, or the use of framing as a method of political persuasion was being interpreted as manipulation.

But is it? Doesn't every effective speechwriter, regardless of their political leaning, employ exactly these techniques? Didn't Lincoln? Didn't JFK and King? Framing is simply science; it's how human brains work. Is it out-of-bounds to employ it in accurately get one's message across?

Lakoff summarizes frames as "mental structures that shape the way we see the world." They are neither left nor right; they're simply there. And we are all carrying around many frames, often covering the same domain; it isn't manipulation to take care to use words that steer your message into the frame you intend. It's stupid, in fact, not to.

"Conservatives understand that rationality doesn't work," he wrote in 2023. "They understand that people actually think in terms of frames and metaphors and images and emotions. So they're great at marketing their ideas, even when they're not based on facts."
A final point, this one from Hartmann: liberals try to engage the mind, while conservatives try to engage emotions; liberals talk facts, conservatives tell stories. The intuitive advantage of the conservative messaging is that human brains become emotionally engaged first, intellectually engaged thereafter; and the human brain's ancient roots are in storytelling, while recitation of fact is relatively new in history.

Liberals, then, are employing a losing strategy when they fail to learn from how conservatives communicate.

It's not tough to learn these principles and commit to them; and it's long past time the left got its act together, and started truly using their words...

"This country is an idea, and one that's lit the world for two centuries and treason against that idea is not just a crime against the living! This ground holds the graves of people who died for it, who gave what Lincoln called the last full measure of devotion."

~Sam

"The best argument against democracy is five minutes with the average voter."

The Voters

Many things are close to Josh Lyman's heart. Voters aren't one of them.

We get hints of this in "Hartsfield's Landing",[11] when he sends Donna outside the White House to call the Flenders family to persuade them not to vote for Rob Ritchie. We see it in "Guns Not Butter",[12] when he has the following exchange with Will:

"The people, in their enduring wisdom, have put in office a chief executive of one party and a Congress of another," Will reads from a speech he's writing. "It's our duty to respect and enact-"

"Strike 'in their enduring wisdom,'" Josh recommends. "You think electing a reactionary Congress and a progressive President was wise? The people, in a fog of uncertainty, unsure of the difference, split tickets across the country."

"Well, I agree, but I think Toby would say that lacks poetry."

"Sixty-eight percent say we hand out too much, 59 percent want to see it cut... So, if we're lucky, foreign aid's going to be funded for another 90 days at 75 cents on the dollar. No one who's ever said they wanted bipartisanship has ever meant it. But the people are speaking. Because 68% think we give too much in foreign aid, and 59% think it should be cut."

"You like that stat?"

"I do. Because nine percent think it's too high, and *shouldn't* be cut! Nine percent of respondents could not fully get their arms around the question. There should be another box you can check for,

---

[11] S3E14.

[12] S4E12.

'I have utterly no idea what you're talking about. Please, god, don't ask for my input.'"

Will isn't exactly wild about American voters himself, as he indicates in this exchange with his stepsister Elsie:[13]

"Does it bother you that for all the legitimate politician bashing, the voters themselves are no bargains?" he asks her. "They think you can have more spending and cut taxes at the same time."

"Listen, when we were kids you would never shut up about the Founders and the Framers and the Fathers," she replies. "This is what they wanted."

"I may never have shut up but clearly you weren't listening much, because the Founders were scared to death of the people."

"They gave them the guns."

"You know that picture in the main stairway of Dad's father with Churchill? He said the best argument against democracy was five minutes with the average voter."

"Grandpa said that?"

"Churchill."

Sorkin and his characters project the belief that the cure for dumb voters is making them better informed, which is a position generally held by Democrats and liberals. There's a seldom-spoken assumption that voters can be won over with facts. To wit:

"The President was at the debate site, walking the stage," says Leo to his attorney, Jordan Kendall.[14] "A podium is a holy place for him. He makes it his own like it's an extension of his body. You ever see a pitcher work the mound so the dirt does exactly what his feet want it to do? That's the President. He sees it as a genuine opportunity to change minds - also his best way of contributing to the team."

Or this, from Joey Lucas, as she and Josh break down polling data:[15]

---

[13] Ibid.

[14] In "Bartlet for America", S3E9.

[15] In "The War at Home", S2E14.

"A five-day waiting period, that's all," Josh says. "A person can't wait five days to buy a gun? If someone needs a gun right now, right this second, isn't that something the public should be concerned about?"

"They're just preliminary numbers," Joey says through Kenny, her interpreter.

"They're not gonna change," he replies.

"It tested well nationwide."

"I didn't need nationwide. I needed those five districts. Now we're gonna have to dial down the gun rhetoric in the Midwest."

"Why not dial it up?"

"Numbers don't lie."

"They lie all the time! They lie when 72% of Americans say they're tired of a sex scandal, while all the while, newspaper circulation goes through the roof for anyone featuring the story.

"You say that these numbers mean dial it down. I say they mean dial it up. You haven't gotten through. There are people you haven't persuaded yet. These numbers mean dial it up. Otherwise, you're like the French radical watching the crowd run by and saying, 'There go my people, I must find out where they are going so I can lead them.'"

These scenes demonstrate an endearing, if somewhat naïve, belief that facts and reason win. And before the Internet and social media, before the era of Trump and MAGA, it was easier to be that brightly optimistic.

But even in the years before *The West Wing*, cognitive scientists like George Lakoff (whom we met above) were working feverishly to demonstrate to us that this just isn't true. It *should* be true - we very much *want* it to be true – but voters very often make the choices they do for reasons they really shouldn't.

Certainly there are many clear-eyed, level-headed voters in the electorate who *can* be persuaded by facts and reason, and hopefully that group includes everyone reading this book. But such people do not constitute a majority of voters. Most voters *don't* cast their votes based on facts and reason.

Self-interest vs. Identity

We heard from linguist/cognitive scientist George Lakoff of Berkeley above, learning that how an argument is framed is at least as important as its actual substance. Now he adds something new:

"People do not necessarily vote in their self-interest. They vote their identity," he wrote in *Don't Think of an Elephant! The Essential Guide for Progressives*. "They vote their values. They vote for who they identify with. They may identify with their self-interest. That can happen. It is not that people never care about their self-interest. But they vote their identity. And if their identity fits their self-interest, they will vote for that. It is important to understand that point.

"Voters vote their identities, not their self-interest," he continued. "Because of the way they frame the world, voters vote in a way that best accords with their identities and not in accord with their self-interest. That is why it is of no use for Democrats to keep pointing out that Bush's tax cuts go to the top 1 percent, not to most voters. If they identify with Bush because they share his culture and his world view, they will vote against their self-interest.

"We saw this in California in the recall election, when, for example, union members overwhelming favored Gray Davis' policies as being better for them, yet voted for Schwarzenegger."

Lakoff points out that, as in the case of framing, conservatives are already firmly in tune with this truth, while liberals just don't get it.

"Conservatives understand that rationality doesn't work," he wrote. "They understand that people actually think in terms of frames and metaphors and images and emotions. So they're great at marketing their ideas, even when they're not based on facts.

"Through constant repetition, they have falsely framed the Republican party as superior on economic matters - despite decades of facts proving otherwise. They have framed this false idea in millions of brains. And when the facts don't fit the frame, they bounce right off.

"Until Democrats and progressives learn and embrace cognitive science, they will continue to lose ground to the false framing imposed by Republicans."

These ideas are not unique to Lakoff, of course. These truths have been out there for a very long time.

"Voters are basically lazy," according to one of Nixon's advisors. "Reason requires a high degree of discipline, of concentration; impression is easier. Reason pushes the viewer back, it assaults him, it demands that he agree or disagree; impression can envelop him, invite him in, without making an intellectual demand; when we argue with him, we seek to engage his intellect; the emotions are more easily roused, closer to the surface, more malleable."

Lee McIntyre puts it another way in "How to Talk to a Science Denier", published in *Skeptical Inquirer*.

"You don't convince someone who doesn't hold their beliefs based on evidence by giving them more evidence. This is called the *information deficit model*, and it doesn't always work. So, we need a more strategic approach."

Adolf Hitler kept it much simpler, saying, "What good fortune for those in power, that people do not think."

Righteous Minds

Social psychologist Jonathan Haidt adds some additional perspective to our understanding of the average voter with his Moral Foundations Theory, crafted with his colleagues Craig Joseph and Jesse Graham. Summarized in his book *The Righteous Mind*, this theory goes a long way in explaining the behaviors and decision-making of partisans.

The basic idea is that there is explicit, codifiable variation in human reasoning that is based on innate psychological foundations. These foundations represent measurable scales that clarify the attitudes of individuals:

- Care/Harm
- Fairness/Cheating
- Loyalty/Betrayal
- Authority/Subversion
- Purity/Degradation

The Care and Fairness foundations represent an *individualizing* cluster, per Haidt, while the Loyalty, Authority and Purity foundations represent a *binding* cluster. Put another way, the latter cluster is about groups, while the former is personal.

These five foundations formed the original version of the theory, but a sixth foundation was added in response to complaints by economic conservatives that the model did not capture their concept of fairness accurately. Haidt responded by adding a new one:

- Liberty/Oppression

The nuance here is that economic conservatives view fairness as a matter of proportionality, not equality, and that fairness should be based on what people have earned.

It is easy to see the roots of political ideology in these moral foundations. With their Moral Foundations Questionnaire, Haidt and Graham were able to determine that liberals are most sensitive to the Care and Fairness cluster, while conservatives are more sensitive than liberals to the Loyalty/Authority/Purity cluster:

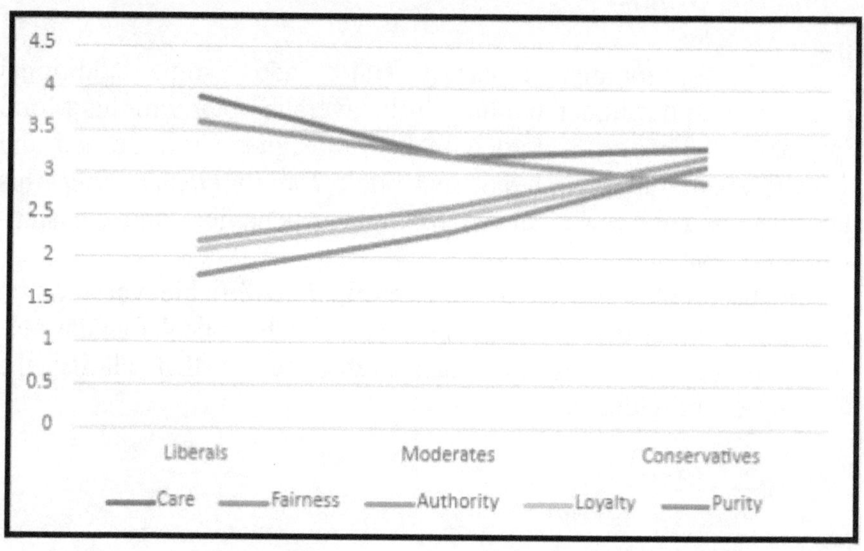

The moral foundations of political affiliation (Haidt et al)

Haidt asserted that these distinctions between groups have a profound impact on our national discourse and the relationships between our two political parties. Each group tends to be blind to one or more of the moral axes of the other, leading to unduly emotional characterizations and misattribution of motivations. An awareness of Moral Foundations Theory among voters, he has argued, could alleviate some of this conflict and misunderstanding, allowing each side to better understand the other.

We don't want to accept that this is how it really is – that so many of us are simply beyond convincing, beyond the reach of fact, immovable from entrenched ideas and beliefs and impressions that are wildly wrong. We want fact and reason to be afforded the impact and influence they deserve, our go-to defaults, and we want those to be the tools by which we all decide, and through which we share in the experience of our collective self-governance.

But the years since *The West Wing* left the air have given us hard lessons in just how far off the reservation some voters can be led. It's more than a little frightening to realize that thousands of our neighbors can become convinced that the fix is in, a shadow government holds sway over us all, and Trump is a victim. And the images of Jan. 6, now firmly fixed in all our minds, underscore that dread all too emphatically.

And yet we can't let go of Jed Bartlet's dogged optimism; some minds *can* be changed by a well-reasoned presentation of fact; some voters *can* find inspiration in unexpected places, and make new choices. Joey Lucas is right; there's a time and a place when it's important to dial it up, not down, and shout your message from the rooftops.

We can't reach everyone; but those we can reach are worthy of our best efforts.

"Today, for the first time in history, the largest group of Americans living in poverty are children. One in five children live in the most abject, dangerous, hopeless, back-breaking, gut-wrenching poverty any of us could imagine. One in five, and they're children. If fidelity to freedom and democracy is the code of our civic religion, then surely the code of our humanity is faithful service to that unwritten commandment that says we shall give our children better than we ourselves received. Let me put it this way: I voted against the bill because I didn't want to make it harder for people to buy milk. I stopped some money from flowing into your pocket. If that angers you, if you resent me, I completely respect that. But if you expect anything different from the president of the United States, you should vote for someone else."

~President Bartlet

That Giant Sucking Sound

Free Trade

Jed Bartlet is a Nobel Prize-winning economist. And, like most economists, he's an advocate of *free trade*.

This is a sufficiently big deal that we hear about it many times. For instance...

Josh and Toby are sitting in the Roosevelt Room with some Democratic congressmen, discussing the Global Free Trade Markets Access Act:[16]

"Josh, we're Democrats," says one of the congressmen. "Since when do we like lower taxes?"

"We don't. We like lower tariffs," Josh replies. "Lower tariffs on everything from Indian textiles, to German cars to Chilean wines negotiated by our trade reps in Geneva with 130 other countries over the past 7 years. Global Free Trade Markets Access Act now has cleared the President and we're very proud it's finally ready to be voted on by the House."

"Where it will win by the way by some 15 votes," Toby adds.

"Now, what happens when you lower the cost of something, economists of every stripe - including the one in the Oval Office - say that you get a more efficient allotment of economic resources. Now that may not sound like much to you and me, but to an economist that's a week in St. Barts."

"Josh, there's no reason to talk to us like we're 12," says the congressman.

"Josh, we're very concerned about the effect cheaper goods flowing into this country will have on American Labor and American Manufacturing," says the other congressman. "We're concerned about the lack of environmental controls."

"Concerns which are entirely reasonable," says the first congressman.

---

[16] In "The White House Pro-Am", S1E17.

"You're concerned about American labor and manufacturing?" Toby asks. "What kind of car do you drive?"

"A Toyota."

"Then shut up."

It's Big Block of Cheese Day once again, and Leo assigns Toby to conduct a "free exchange of ideas" with a group of 100 protesters at a World Policy Studies forum. Toby is less than thrilled. When he arrives, he finds that a DC police officer has been assigned to look after him. Since the protesters are too noisy and disorderly to speak to, he chats with the officer.[17]

"Since you're not really doing anything right now," the officer says, "I was wondering, what's this all about?"

"It's about the WTO, Rhonda, the World Trade Organization," he replies.

"Well, I get that from the signs and the newspapers."

"The World Trade Organization's a group of 140 countries who have agreed to specific trade policies."

"So, what's wrong with that?"

"Nothing's wrong with that."

"What would they say if I asked them the same question?" she asks, motioning toward the chaotic protesters.

"They'd say the WTO benefits corporations and not people," he answers.

"Does it?"

"It benefits both," he replies.

Their conversation continues when Toby, bored, walks outside and she follows.

"It's activist vacation is what it is. Spring break for anarchist wannabes. The black t-shirts, the gas masks as fashion accessories."

"These kids today," she mocks him, "with the hair and the clothes..."

"All right, that's it, flatfoot. You want the benefits of free trade? Food is cheaper. Food is cheaper, clothes are cheaper, steel is

---

[17] In "Somebody's Going to Emergency, Somebody's Going to Jail", S2E16.

cheaper, cars are cheaper, phone service is cheaper. You feel me building a rhythm here? That's 'cause I'm a speechwriter and I know how to make a point.

"It lowers prices, it raises income. You see what I did with *lowers* and *raises* there? It's called the science of listener attention. We did repetition, we did floating opposites and now you end with the one that's not like the others. Ready? *Free trade stops wars.* And that's it. Free trade stops wars! And we figure out a way to fix the rest! One world, one peace. I'm sure I've seen that on a sign somewhere."

"God, Toby... Wouldn't it be great if there was someone around here with communication skills who could go in there and tell them that?"

And, again, Toby says,

"Shut up."

President Bartlet's re-election day has just begun, and the community of Hartsfield's Landing (population 63), in his native New Hampshire, has a long record of voting for the winner in every presidential contest. He and the staff have been there, and he keeps sending Donna out into the evening cold to talk to the Flenders family of Hartsfield's Landing, to see who they will be voting for when they cast their ballots just after midnight on election day.[18]

"How'd it go?" Josh asks her when she returns the first time.

"They're not voting for us."

"Why?"

"Because the old Perren pulp mill is still idle after five years."

"It's been five years, and why is it our fault?"

"Because instead of protecting American jobs we're letting Canadian pulp importers take over their market share."

"It's called free trade."

"It's also called 'why the Flenders aren't voting for us'."

---

[18] In "Hartsfield's Landing", S3E14.

President Bartlet is about to debate his Republican challenger, Rob Ritchie, and the long-serving Assistant Secretary of State Albie Duncan, a Republican, will be helping CJ with spin for the press afterwards. They sit on Air Force One, running through some of the answers he will give.[19]

"Trade is essential for human rights," Albie says. "Instead of isolating them, we make them live by the same global trading rules as everyone else and gain 1.2 billion consumers for our products and strengthen the forces of reform."

"That's it. It's that simple," CJ replies.

"No, it's not simple, it's incredibly complicated," he disagrees. "McGarry's boy's over there coming up with greeting cards."

"Josh?"

"He's sitting with me, trying to boil down foreign policy into a ten-word statement."

"And believe me, he hates it," CJ says.

"I've been at the State Department for 30 years and there's no right answer for these questions and diplomacy needs all the words it can get its hands on. Plus, he's from Connecticut."

"Yes."

"The answer I just gave you on trade? You know there's a decent chance I'm full of crap, right?"

"Sure."

"'Free trade is essential for human rights'... the end of that sentence is 'we hope, because nothing else has worked.'"

Another big international free trade agreement has come up and President Bartlet is preparing to fly to Brussels to sign it. The staff have been energetically prepping for the many discussions and interviews to come, while dealing with an accumulation of tractor-driving protestors outside the White House.[20]

Larry and Ed discuss the messaging with Josh in the Roosevelt Room, showing him a talking point they've written:

---

[19] In "Game On", S4E6.

[20] In "Talking Points", S5E19.

"That's not the message."

"'Protecting intellectual property through international copyright enforcement,'" Ed reads.

"Okay, I know what you're talking about, and I don't know what you're talking about."

"Isn't that what we-"

"Free trade creates jobs! It creates better, higher-paying jobs. We still have to pass this through Congress."

"What are European farmers so upset about?" Donna asks him later.

"That they can't cling to a dying way of life, that free trade means that some of them might have to wear neckties, that they can't beat Pentium chips back into plowshares. Take your pick."

"What do you say to the opponents of free trade, people who say it exports jobs?" CJ asks the president later.

"That giant sucking sound," Josh adds.

"Any half-decent economist will tell you to wear earplugs," Bartlet replies, "then file immediately for unemployment.

"Hey, listen," he explains. "Any economic advancement involves what Schumpeter called 'creative destruction.'"

"Not a good answer."

"Why?"

"Because that word 'destruction' will really mollify our critics."

"Free trade creates jobs," Josh repeats.

"Selling our products to the world," CJ smirks.

Even staff latecomer Will Bailey is on board:[21]

"With midterms coming up, what do you think?" Josh asks him. "How'd you become a free trader?"

"America has a quarter of the world's wealth and only two percent of the customers. You have to sell to others."

"So, how do you make that case to people who are about to lose their jobs?"

---

[21] Ibid.

"Ask them how often they go to Wal-Mart to buy cheap cardigans or drill-bits."

"Drill-bits?"

"I don't wear cardigans. But I like a nice drill-bit."

"So it all comes down to cheap drill-bits."

"Pay more for a drill-bit, you have less to spend on other things," Will replies. "Keep out cheap, foreign drill-bits, that country'll keep out cheap American something else. And that costs us jobs."

"Do you ever wonder if we forget the human face of trade, the blood and muscle?"

"You have to go with what grows the economy for everyone. There's blood and muscle in India, too... So how'd you become a free trader?"

"I came to work for one."

Neoliberalism

Okay, lots and lots of love of *free trade* in the Bartlet White House. And that love has implications broad and deep.

To begin with, free trade is perhaps the most complex issue the show persistently tackles, and it's unquestionably the one with the murkiest political threads. Let's begin with a simple definition:

free trade is *unregulated trade*

Right away, hot buttons are pushed. *Unregulated* is a word that capitalists tend to love and liberals/progressives tend to distrust. On the other hand, deregulating trade opens international doors for a more balanced and equitable global economy, which liberals/progressives love, and nationalists and America First conservatives tend to hate.

Among free trade advocates, there will be both liberals and conservatives. And, among opponents of unregulated trade, there will be both liberals and conservatives.

That makes the landscape *very* complicated. But it's more complicated still.

Free trade as we think of it today was a policy created and advocated by a group of European and American economists, businessmen and politicians in the aftermath of World War II, convening to conceive a firewall between Western economies and the growing threat of rising communism. This group constructed a new political-economic ideology – *neoliberalism*[22] – that went on to proliferate in both Europe and the US, and which came to dominate American politics and economics with the ascent of Ronald Reagan to the presidency in 1981.

Neoliberalism, as a philosophy, has had such a tremendous impact on the Western world over the past half-century that it has its own appendix in this book. It has its place as the source of the free-trade thinking used by Bartlet and the staff in the show, and of course we see it in the real world, but the deeper implications will be addressed later on.

Free trade is how US industries went to China and elsewhere following the deregulation of the Eighties – something that would have been unthinkable 20 years earlier. Free trade is embodied in the North American Free Trade Agreement of 1994 between the US, Canada, and Mexico, promoted by Presidents Reagan, Bush I, and Clinton.

It achieves all the things claimed above by Josh and Toby, and can be credited with accelerating the economic growth of many nations. And it has lessened the negative impact of *protectionism* – imposition of trade quotas and restrictive tariffs – on the US and other nations that had practiced it in the past.

On the other hand, the negative effects of free trade cited in the scenes above, and railed against by Toby's hapless world policy audience, are both real and prevalent. Free trade creates jobs, but it costs jobs – often tens of thousands or more – up front. Economies get energized – but not everyone benefits from that energy.

Hartmann points out that reducing the government's ability to constrain corporations boosts inequality, causing money to flow upward rather than outward, and can (and almost always does) result

---

[22] Though the word *liberal* is imbedded in this term, the usage is far afield of the US political meaning; here, it's closer to the European usage of *liberal* as meaning *free* – as in *free of government*.

in a social reprioritization that elevates the well-being of business above the well-being of people. This is, in fact, one of the key concerns of life in America in the 21st century; that despite the health of the US economy and the endless boon experienced by the wealthy, the buying power of the average citizen has steadily grown more and more anemic over time. Education, healthcare, home ownership – all have fallen farther and farther out of reach for young adults entering the workforce as the deregulated world of *free trade* has become the universal norm.

To be sure, there has been pushback, and not always from progressive liberals. Donald Trump sought to eliminate NAFTA as one of his first acts in office, with the intent of bullying Canada and Mexico into an agreement more favorable to the US – an intent that is in direct opposition to the entire point of free trade. And pushback emerges from sources of all kinds, politics aside, when Bartlet's *creative destruction* – the clearing-away of economic status quo to make way for new activity – hits in someone's backyard.

The magical market

In neoliberal ideology, the free market is *magical*, according to Reagan. *The magic of the market*, he maintained in speech after speech, could do things government could never do. We should get government out of the way, and let the market work its magic on society – creating here, destroying there.

Bartlet the economist gets faced down by this when tech CEO Jake Kimball, who runs Antares (*The West Wing* equivalent of the real world's Dell), arrives at the White House to announce that a defect has been found in a microprocessor currently deployed in 80 million computers around the world – including throughout US government, and that the company is going to order a recall.[23]

"That's the end of Antares," Bartlet soberly realizes in discussing it with Leo. "Ninety-eight thousand workers, I think 75,000 in the US. Plus the kidney punch at NASDAQ..."

---

[23] In "Enemies Foreign and Domestic", S3E18.

"I think Jake's gonna put a shotgun in his mouth, I really do," Leo replies.

Leo wants to do something to help Antares survive – to have the administration intervene in some way, something the president is philosophically opposed to: it's a cornerstone of neoliberalism that the government should let the market sort itself out.

"The government can't be in the business of cosigning loans."

"We wouldn't be handing them a bag of unmarked bills, just backing the loans to cover the cost of the recall."

"It's a subsidy."

"Sir! This was not a failure of business, it was... I don't know, it was a mistake, it was human error, and Jake's been completely forth-"

"The marketplace will take care of Antares."

"The marketplace will *kill* Antares."

"That's what's supposed to happen."

"It's not like it's unprecedented, sir. We helped out steel."

"That was an industry that was hurt by unfair trade practices. Antares was hurt by their own carelessness."

"A loan guarantee doesn't cost the taxpayers a nickel."

"-unless they go under, and either way we've just said, we're open for business."

"-for a corporate icon that feeds into tech companies, computers, aerospace. The ripple effects, workers losing jobs..."

Leo won't let it go.

"You said it was carelessness and I don't believe carelessness has to exist for a mistake to be made," he tells Bartlet later. "Jake was a contributor, and he's never asked for a favor, not even now. He was a contributor 'cause he knows us, and we know him, and we know, that if a mistake happened in design or production at Antares it wasn't shoddy... it wasn't on the cheap. You know how many chips have acted up so far? *One.* Dollars to donuts, he could have gotten away with it. But he wanted to warn people they may have a problem before... I don't even know what happens when 80 million computers stop working right. But tell me this isn't *exactly* how we want American business to behave!"

In the end, Bartlet confronts this contradiction and realizes it isn't just a matter of cold doctrine; he finds a way to help. While he won't provide the backing for a loan to support the Antares recall, he tells Jake Kimball that he can count on the US government remaining his biggest customer.

Creative destruction

Finally, Josh's chickens come home to roost in his international free trade deal with its tractor protests and drill bits. Behind his back, a major big tech firm makes a deal with India – one of the signatories of the new trade agreement – to export thousands of jobs to that country, once the patent protections Josh negotiated are in force.

Josh is aghast. It means thousands of computer professionals suddenly unemployed in the US, and it's on him.

Creative destruction.

Josh sits down with one of the big tech firm's lobbyists:[24]

"The CWA says you're shipping 17,000 computer programming jobs there."

"That's proprietary information."

"Then why's India signing this trade deal? India, which hated the agricultural provisions, hated the light industrial provisions..."

"There's a chance JCN will be moving some jobs there."

"You can't do this! After everything I negotiated for you?"

"You toughened copyright enforcement. Now it's safer for us to move sensitive programming work overseas."

"Over time, fine. But not overnight. We worked together for months without one word about this."

"It's an internal business decision."

"Yet, somehow, the nation of India, population 1 billion and rising, slipped into a JCN board meeting?"

"We lobbied through our trade association. That's how these things work."

---

[24] In "Talking Points", S5E19.

"No. When I help you on a trade deal, you don't lobby behind my back. That's how these things work."

"It's economics."

"It's politics, and you know it! Now I got a union problem. When they go nuts, I got a Congressional problem."

"We'll help you lobby. We're good at that."

"It's not gonna pass! 17,000 flesh-and-blood families, spread over who-knows-how-many Congressional districts."

"It's more like 3.3 million jobs, over the next ten years. Industry-wide, of course... American programmers make 40 bucks an hour. In India, it's 10. This is how free trade works. You can't be surprised jobs moving overseas."

"Yeah, but they'd only be this big. I need you to spread the layoffs over a couple years."

"We're a business, not a halfway house."

"Is that what you told the head of your union?"

"No. But feel free to tell him yourself. I'm sure he's on his way over here right now."

So Josh the free trader has to sit down with representatives of the computer programmers' union that's about to get hit and tell them their jobs are going away, and there's nothing he can do, because free trade. He gets his first real look at that human face of trade, the blood and muscle.

It all sounds great on paper, but when economic policy becomes doctrine, when nuance is eschewed and that human face is obscured, its promise goes unrealized and its ultimate intent is lost to more individual concerns. Josh and the president have both learned that the doctrines they've embraced can't be couched in absolutes; there needs to be a reading between the lines, and a recognition of the nuance.

And that goes for us, too.

"Education is the silver bullet! Education is everything. We don't need little changes, we need gigantic monumental changes! Schools should be palaces! The competition for the best teachers should be fierce. They should be making six-figure salaries! School should be incredibly expensive for government and absolutely free of charge to its citizens, just like national defense! That's my position."

~Sam

"Not only were the shooters white; they were doing it because one of us wasn't."

Race

The West Wing got into the issue of race time and again – and always to great effect.

One of the earliest – and most memorable, from the standpoint of fantastic guest performances – occurred in "Celestial Navigation",[25] when Supreme Court nominee Roberto Mendoza is jailed in a small Connecticut town, allegedly for drunk driving. Sam and Toby are dispatched to spring him before it becomes public.

"Why didn't you take a Breathalyzer?" Toby asks Mendoza when they are alone in the jail cell.

"Because I was driving within the speed limit, I was driving on the right side of the road, I had valid tags and registration and as far as I know, I don't have any warrants for my arrest in Connecticut. Absent just cause, Toby, the Breathalyzer's an illegal search. It's a civil rights violation."

"So you give Barney Fife a hard time to make a point."

"A point worth making."

"One phone call, judge! 'Toby, this has happened. Tell 'em my name's Roberto Mendoza and the President's named me to the bench!'"

"They pulled me over because I look like my name is Roberto Mendoza and I'm coming to rob your house."

Then there's Josh's meeting with Jeff Breckinridge, whom the White House wants to appoint Assistant Attorney General for Civil

---

[25] S1E15.

Rights, hamstrung by a blurb he wrote for a book on civil war reparations:[26]

"You wrote, 'Otis Hastings is a unique and extraordinary historian. This book should be read by everyone and burned into the minds of white America.' Just to start, you weren't misquoted, right?"

"No."

"Okay. And I'm assuming that if asked by the committee, you'll say that you favor reparations?"

"If asked, I'll tell the committee that my father's fathers were kidnapped outside a village called Wimbabwa, brought to New Guinea, sold to a slave trader from Boston and bought by a plantation owner in Wadsworth, South Carolina, where they worked for no wages."

"And you're looking for back pay?"

"Yes."

"Just out of curiosity, did you have a figure in mind?"

"Dr. Harold Washington, who's chief economist at the Manchester Institute, calculated the number of slaves held, multiplied it by the number of hours worked, multiplied that by the market value of manual labor and came up with a very conservative figure."

"What is it?"

"One point seven trillion dollars. Someone owes me and my friends 1.7 trillion dollars."

On the more frivolous side: President Bartlet learns that his youngest daughter Zoey wants to date his body man, Charlie - who is, of course, black:[27]

"Got a racial problem?" Leo asks his boss.

"A racial problem?"

"It's okay to admit it."

---

[26] In "Six Meetings Before Lunch", S1E18.

[27] In "Lord John Marbury", S1E11.

"I don't! I'm Spencer Tracy at the *end* of *Guess Who's Coming to Dinner*! My problem isn't that she's white and he's black; it's that she's a girl and he's not. To say nothing of he's older than she is."

"She's 19, he's 21."

"Yeah, but a guy learns a lot in those two years."

It's not so frivolous a few weeks later:[28]

"It's time for me to tell you about some letters we've been getting," Bartlet tells Zoey in the White House residence. "They don't like that the daughter of the President is dating a young black man."

"Charlie?"

"Zoey, please don't tell me you're dating more than one guy."

"How bad are the letters?"

"No worse than any of the stuff they intercept."

"Except these are from white supremacists?"

"Yeah."

The upshot is that Zoey and Charlie are planning on going to a club opening the following weekend, and the Secret Service has advised against it.

Zoey tells Charlie they can't go, because of the death threats.

"I don't give a damn! I bought a new suit!"

"Charlie, we can't go."

Charlie looks down at a book Donna has loaned Zoey about life a century ago.

"Hey, look," he says. "It says here that a hundred years ago a black guy couldn't show up to a club opening with a white girl for fear he'd be killed."

Not long after, President Bartlet and his entourage – including both Charlie and Zoey – are in Rosslyn, Virginia, where he has given a talk at the Newseum. There is gunfire, as two members of West Virginia White Pride open fire. Bartlet and Josh are wounded – the latter, critically – and the shooters are dispatched by Secret Service, later apprehending their accomplice.

Charlie is brought to the recuperating Bartlet's hospital room, where Ron Butterfield, head of his Secret Service detail, is waiting:[29]

---

28 In "The White House Pro-Am", S1E17.

"Excuse me, sir, I was told you wanted to see me?"

"Yeah," Bartlet answers. "Charlie, the guy the Secret Service has in custody is named Carl Leroy. He gives a statement in which he says that he and the two shooters were members of an organization called West Virginia White Pride."

"They tried to kill the President 'cause Zoey and I are together?"

"Charlie, the president wasn't the target. According to the statement, the president wasn't the target."

There is a long moment as it sinks in.

Finally, the White House is on lock-down: a terrorist has been taken into custody crossing into Vermont from Canada, and in turning state's evidence to the US Attorney, he named a co-conspirator – Raqim Ali. There are three Raqim Alis in the country, and one of them works in the West Wing.[30]

He is detained and questioned by Leo and Ron Butterfield.

"You went to Edison High School in Patterson, correct?" asks one of Butterfield's men.

"Correct?"

"On December 3, 1994, someone called in a bomb threat to the school."

"Yeah, I remember that there were bomb threats. I remember that there were more than one, but I don't remember the exact dates."

"According to your transcripts, police questioned you."

"Yeah, it's on my school transcript 'cause I wasn't arrested. They asked if I called in a bomb threat, which I didn't. It was a couple of football players that didn't want to take a chem final."

"So it was a couple of football players, but they called you in anyway?"

"It's not uncommon for Arab Americans to be the first suspected when that sort of thing happens."

---

[29] In "In the Shadow of Two Gunmen, Pt. II", S2E2.

[30] In "Isaac and Ishmael", the Season 3 special opening episode.

"I can't imagine why," Leo interjects. "I'm trying to figure out why anytime there's any terrorist activity, people always assume it's Arabs. I'm racking my brain."

"I don't know the answer to that, Mr. McGarry, but I can tell you it's horrible."

"Well, that's the price you pay," Leo almost sneers.

Ali is enraged.

"Excuse me? The price I pay for what?"

Leo's unseemly hostility turns to bleak humility when the actual Raqim Ali the FBI is seeking is located abroad, and Ron tells the innocent West Wing staffer he is free to go.

"You have the memory of a gypsy moth," Ali tells Leo as he departs. "When you and the President and the President's daughter and about a hundred other people - including me, by the way - were met with a hail of .44-calibre gunfire in Rosslyn, not only were the shooters white... they were doing it because one of us wasn't."

The West Wing special episode "Isaac and Ishmael" was hastily written and produced as an unexpected third season opener in the aftermath of 9/11. As such, the theme of race was a natural and appropriate one, as the US had just been attacked by terrorists of Arab origin, resulting in backlash against Arabs all across the country.

According to the FBI Uniform Crime Reporting Program,[31] prior to 9/11, the most frequent hate crimes in the US were religion-based, followed by hate crimes motivated by bias against sexual orientation. The fewest number of hate crimes were driven by ethnicity or national-origin bias.

> "That distribution changed in 2001, presumably as a result
> of the heinous incidents that occurred on September 11,"
> according to the program report. "For many offenders, the
> preformed negative opinion, or bias, was directed toward
> ethnicity/ national origin. Consistent with past data, by bias

---

[31] https://ucr.fbi.gov/hate-crime/2001/hatecrime01.pdf

type, law enforcement reported that most incidents in 2001 were motivated by bias against race. However, crime incidents motivated by bias against ethnicity/national origin were the second most frequently reported bias in 2001, more than doubling the number of incidents, offenses, victims, and known offenders from 2000 data. Additionally, the anti-other ethnicity/national origin category quadrupled in incidents, offenses, victims, and known offenders.

"Another noticeable increase in 2001 was among religious-bias incidents. Anti-Islamic religion incidents were previously the second least reported, but in 2001, they became the second highest reported among religious-bias incidents (anti-Jewish religion incidents were the highest), growing by more than 1,600 percent over the 2000 volume. In 2001, reported data showed there were 481 incidents made up of 546 offenses having 554 victims of crimes motivated by bias toward the Islamic religion."

Hate crimes against Muslims to their highest level ever, increasing 1,617%, according to the FBI.[32]

Beyond Islamophobia and its conjured association with terrorism, race is a big deal on *The West Wing* because, historically and in the present day, it's a big deal for America. Lord John Marbury tells Toby in "Dead Irish Writers" that "For Americans, it's slavery. Slavery is your original sin. That and your unfortunate history with your aborigines."[33] In "The Short List", Sam lists civil rights as the nation's most serious concern during the Fifties and Sixties.[34]

As the radical right has pushed into authoritarian territory over the past 15 years, it has leveraged racial tension to rile up its base.

---

[32] https://www.pewresearch.org/short-reads/2017/11/15/assaults-against-muslims-in-u-s-surpass-2001-level/

[33] S3E15.

[34] S1E9.

The result has been an upsurge in race-related incidents across the board – including, tragically, police brutality, as in the murder of George Floyd by a Minneapolis police officer in May 2020.

Some of the all-too-common mass shootings of recent years have been race-driven, as in the August 2023 murders of three black victims in a Dollar General store in Jacksonville, Florida, by a masked white man with a swastika on his gun.

Violence toward blacks seems as reflexive as it was a hundred years ago. In April 2018, 14-year-old Brennan Walker, a young black man, was shot in a Detroit suburb simply for asking directions, after knocking on the door of retired firefighter Jeffrey Zeigler.

Donald Trump, of course, has been the source of much of the right's renewed animus toward people of other ethnicities, starting with his 2017 executive order banning immigrants from several Islamic nations.

Racial tension has always been part of the American story, and Lord John was correct in saying that slavery is our original sin. What is most distressing about the here-and-now is that since *The West Wing* left the air, we've returned to the place we were two generations ago, the age of right-wingers like the segregationist Sen. Strom Thurmond of South Carolina, who vehemently opposed the 1964 Civil Rights Act and the 1965 Voting Rights Act. The Roberts Court, with its conservative majority, gutted the latter in 2013, opening the door to a return to the days of black voter disenfranchisement. To a certain degree, we're right back where we started.

Except... we now count a black man among our past presidents.

The current vice-president is a black woman.

We've seen the first Muslim elected to Congress – Representative Keith Ellison, Minnesota Democrat – in 2007. In 2018, two Muslim women followed – Democratic Representatives Ilhan Omar and Rashida Tlaib.

We have the most ethnically diverse Congress in history, with 133 members who are black, Hispanic, Asian-American, or Native America, according to the Pew Research Center and the Congressional Research Service.

The racial problems of the US are among those issues Jed Bartlet was talking about in conversation with Abbey:[35]

"German thinker Max Weber said that politics is the 'slow boring of hard boards and that anyone who seeks to do it must risk his own soul'… It means that change comes in excruciating increments for those who want it. You're trying to move mountains. It takes lifetimes."

It surely seems so.

---

[35] In "Privateers", S4E18.

"In the future, if you're wondering, 'Crime - boy, I don't know' is when I decided to kick your ass."

~President Bartlet

"We can all get together on the grenade launcher, right?"

Gun Control

The West Wing was always big on the issue of gun control, and that's because Aaron Sorkin himself was big on it: it was one of the two central issues in *The American President*, the show's cinematic template, and it appeared again and again.

It was the first major legislative showdown we got to see - in "Five Votes Down", over a gun control bill the White House was strongly pushing (and which cost Leo his marriage).[36] This episode gave us several big pieces of the gun control puzzle.

First, Josh learns that freshman Congressman Chris Wick, whom Josh got elected, is voting against the bill. He points out to Wick that the PCR and NFR (models of automatic weapons) are just copycats of the AR-15, which has already been banned (a familiar move of the gun industry; if the gun is banned, just make another one like it and call it something else). And that the Pat Maxi is a grenade launcher.

"You know, I realize as an adult not everyone shares my view of the world," he says to Wick. "And with an issue as hot as gun control I'm prepared to accept a lot of different points of view as being perfectly valid. But we can all get together on the *grenade launcher*, right?"

He also learns that Wick isn't aware of any of this because he hasn't even read the bill; he's voting against it purely for political leverage.

Then there's Leo's meeting with black caucus leader Mark Richardson, who rebuffs Leo because he considers the bill as it stands to be a weak compromise that does little to protect his constituents.

---

[36] S1E4.

"We have to do this inch by inch," Leo tells him. "You know how this works."

"No, I know how you guys work."

"That is out of line, Congressman. Guns are number one on my list of priorities and I've never moved the President off of that. God, Mark! The bodies being wheeled into the emergency room are black! These guns aren't going to Scottsdale, Mark, they're going to Detroit, they're going to Philadelphia. An entire generation of African American men are being eaten alive by drugs and poverty."

"Well, I'm encouraged to hear the White House has discovered there's a drug problem in this country. I mean your penetrating insight is matched only by the courage displayed in the authorship of this bill. Not the three-inch grip, but the two-inch grip. With the forty-gauge barrel and the thirty-round clip, not the twenty-round clip. With a three-day wait to run a check to see if you're crazy. As if wanting the gun wasn't a pretty good heads-up in the first place.

"No, this is for show. And I think it's an unconscionable waste of the taxpayer's money to have it printed, signed and photocopied, to say nothing of enforced. No, I want the guns, Leo. You write a law that can save some lives, I'll sign it. In the meantime, please don't tell me how to be a leader of black men. You look like an idiot."

So, many who vote in favor of guns don't even realize what they're specifically voting for, and the incrementalism of progress on this issue is frustrating and offensive to those who are most victimized by unregulated weapons in the marketplace.

Sorkin adds another wrinkle in a conversation between President Bartlet and John Hoynes, a former Texas senator whom he wants to send there to speak for him after a church shooting in that state.[37] Hoynes doesn't want to go, because he knows that taking an anti-gun stance will be very politically damaging to him.

"You know, last month in Idaho, a man killed six members of his family, including his pregnant wife. And you know why the liberal intelligentsia didn't go crazy? Because he did it with an ax. You think we need ax control?"

On and on they argue.

---

[37] In "War Crimes", S3E5.

"We can't all just agree it's a stupid-ass amendment that was written before there were street lamps, much less police forces, and move on?" Bartlet asks. "There's no need for a citizen militia."

"Forty percent of Americans have a gun in their home," Hoynes counters.

"Only 16% believe gun ownership is an absolute right. Only 9% believe it's an absolute wrong. There's a middle. We can win them!"

But it's Toby who really brings it home, in an on-air confrontation with Congressman Henry Shallick during a telecast of *Capital Beat*, live from the White House, on the night of President Bartlet's third State of the Union address:[38]

"Excuse me," Shallick says to Toby, "but this White House uses the first amendment to protect flag burning, to protect pornography, to ban school prayer. Why, when the second amendment clearly says that the federal government will not infringe upon a citizen's-"

"It doesn't say that at all," Toby interrupts. "The only way it says that at all is if you remove some words from it. It says a *well-regulated militia*, being necessary for the security of the free state... the government shall not infringe. The words *regulated* and *militia* are in the first sentence. I don't think the Framers were thinking of three guys in a Dodge Durango."

"Well, you don't really know what the Framers were thinking, do you?"

"No. But I do know that if you combine the populations of Great Britain, France, Germany, Japan, Switzerland, Sweden, Denmark and Australia you've got a population roughly the size of the United States. We had 32,000 gun deaths last year and they had 112. Do you think it's because Americans are more homicidal by nature? Or do you think it's because those guys have gun control laws?"

Let's move right past Congressman Shallick being okay with not knowing what the Framers were thinking – as if we should just

---

[38] In "Bartlet's Third State of the Union", S2E13.

follow their writings blindly – and consider the effects of unregulated guns in the US, before and after *The West Wing*.

Thom Hartmann, former psychotherapist turned political commentator, passed along a realization first attributed to criminologist Grant Duwe – that the year 1966 marks a turning point in America's relationship with guns.[39]

For a period of 50 years, from 1916 to 1966, Duwe wrote, the US only experienced 25 mass shootings altogether (lower than today's annual rate). The turning point was one of the most infamous shootings, in which Charles Whitman climbed into the clock tower at the University of Texas and killed 12 people, wounding more than 30 others. Armed with three rifles, four pistols, and more than 700 rounds of ammunition, he determinedly dug in for 96 minutes, eventually shot dead by Austin police officers.

The event that prompted Duwe to make note of that seminal event was a similar shooting in October 2017, when Stephen Paddock fired on concertgoers at the Route 91 Harvest Music Festival in Las Vegas, killing 58 people and wounding 851 others.

Why 1966? Per Hartmann, unprecedented public protest was erupting throughout the country, over both civil rights and the US intervention in Vietnam; activists for civil rights had been shot to death. Nixon had exacerbated a resurgence of violence in the South with his race-baiting "Southern strategy"; Ronald Reagan then fanned the flames with the reactionary economics that disenfranchised tens of millions.[40] And Donald Trump put a bow on the modern era with his relentless hatred toward immigrants, and Mexicans in particular. Since Whitman, it's been open season, and those politicians and others have exploited gun tragedy to misdirect public attention and advance ideological agendas.

Hartmann lists several of the most prominent massacres:

- The McDonald's Massacre in San Ysidro, CA (1984);
- The Edmond, OK post office shooting (1986);

---

[39] In "The Hidden History of Guns and the Second Amendment", by Hartmann.

[40] In his diatribe against the protests at Berkeley, Reagan advocated violence to "clean the mess up": "If it takes a bloodbath, let's get it over with."

- The Luby's Cafeteria Massacre, Killen, TX (1991);
- The Cinema Shooting, Aurora, CO (2012);
- The Sutherland Springs, TX Church Shooting (2017);
- School shootings in Columbine, CO (1999); Sandy Hook, CT (2012); Parkland, FL (2018)

Hartmann goes on to summarize gun violence in a single year – 2018 – as follows:

- The Borderline Bar & Grill shooting in Thousand Oaks, CA on Nov. 7 was the 307th mass shooting of the year, with 13 killed and 16 wounded;
- The tally for the year, per *USA Today*, was at that time 328 killed, more than 1,000 wounded.

It is doubtful that anyone reading this needs any convincing. Gun violence is out of control in the US, and has gotten far, far worse since *The West Wing* was on the air.

But what do we do about it?

Hartmann and others make the point that the guns are a focal point of corruption in US politics; that, to a large degree, legislative action on gun violence is curtailed by money in the pockets of lawmakers. That needs to be addressed, no matter what.

Beyond that, there needs to be a decoupling in the "guns" category: automatic and semi-automatic weapons, rifles designed explicitly to kill soldiers on the battlefield, should not be lumped in with hunting rifles and defensive handguns. That, too, is a stand-alone step that can be taken; the reduction of automatic and semi-automatic weapons in the marketplace will lower the incidence of mass shootings.

Finally, Hartmann suggests that effective regulation of guns can be modeled on the manner in which we regulate cars. Where cars are concerned, the law requires

- *Clear declaration of ownership*; we know exactly who owns which vehicles, and the same should apply to weapons;

- *Competence must be demonstrated*; you cannot operate a vehicle unless you've proven you know how, and the same should apply to weapons;
- Liability insurance is required of car drivers; creating law requiring the same of gun owners would put insurance companies – one of the nation's most powerful lobbies – on the side of regulation.[41]

To make any of these things happen, of course, new laws must be put in place – and that has been the challenge. There will certainly be no come-to-Jesus moments among those who oppose gun control; legal accountability must be put in place, and that only happens when a majority of legislators make it so.

Again, the message is simple: *vote*, and encourage others to do the same.

And though "ax control" and even Toby's excellent summary won't change any minds, we may as well go ahead and use them, anyway; they keep us focused on the issue, and why it's important to put lawmakers in place who can do something about it.

---

[41] Hartmann makes the excellent point that if you drive a car into a crowd and kill a dozen people, your insurance company is on the hook for millions; if you take an AR-15 into a mall and kill a dozen people, no one gets a dime.

"*Can I get some water while you regroup?*"

Abortion

Supreme Court Justice Owen Brady has died, and it falls to President Bartlet to nominate a new justice. In the current political climate, he believes he is limited to nominating a moderate acceptable to the opposition Senate.

Josh and Toby begin talks with possible candidates, and conspire to scare Republicans into accepting their nominee by parading disturbing ones around the White House.

One of these is Evelyn Baker Lang, a staggeringly competent and intelligent jurist whose liberal proclivities are well-known. She is just a shill, and she knows it, but when Josh and Toby speak with her in the Roosevelt Room, Josh is immediately smitten: she is exactly what the court needs.

"Let's talk a little bit about what the judiciary committee's concerns would be," Josh begins. "We can safely say reproductive rights are gonna come up."

"They're going to say judicial activism, particularly in jury," Toby continues. "How would you address that?"

"And you're who?" Lang asks.

"I'm sorry?"

"Who are you? We're playing committee?"

"This will be coming from one of the 11 Republicans."

"If you're Webster, the question is 'Where do you stand on *Roe v. Wade*?'. And the answer is 'Judicial rulings shouldn't be based on personal ideologies - mine or anyone else's'.

"If you're Davies, the question is 'How would you approach the next case?' because he's the drum banger on partial birth. And the answer is 'I don't comment on hypotheticals'.

"If you're Malkin, you're from Virginia, so you're asking *in re: Drury*. I take you point by point from the doctor to the father to Casey to undue burden to equal protection back to *Roe* at which point you can't remember the question, and I drink my water for a minute while you regroup."

Josh and Toby excuse themselves briefly, and Josh practically bounces off the ceiling. He thinks she's perfect. *I love her mind... I love her shoes...*

When they return, he says, "You were vetted by the FBI when you hit the Federal bench, but if we re-opened an investigation-"

"Let's see... in high school, I snuck a copy of *Lady Chatterley's Lover* out of the public library and never returned it. In college, I got a marijuana plant from my roommate as a birthday present. In year two of law school, I had an abortion."

Josh and Toby sit there, stunned.

"Can I get some water while you regroup?"

The abortion issue is a big one in the Bartlet White House. CJ objects to a provision in the Family Wellness Act requiring doctors to counsel women seeking abortions on the adoption alternative.[42] Abbey Bartlet objects to Congressman Clancy Bangart attaching an amendment to a Foreign Ops bill stipulating that the funds it allots cannot go to overseas clinics counseling abortion.[43]

And Amy Gardner, clarifying her love for the president to Josh, makes clear that part of that love is his abortion stance: President Bartlet will defend the right of women to choose:

"The next Justice can overturn *Roe*," she says. "You don't screw around with that."

Needless to say, Amy's worst nightmare came true. On June 24, 2022, the US Supreme Court overturned *Roe v. Wade* after almost 50 years in its *Dobbs v. Jackson Women's Health Organization* decision. The vote was 6-3.

This ruling was particularly egregious, given that three of the Justices voting in favor – Neil Gorsuch, Brett Kavanaugh, and Amy Coney Barrett – were all Trump appointees who disingenuously

---

[42] In "The Stackhouse Filibuster", S2E17.

[43] In "Privateers", S4E18.

declared before Congress that they considered *Roe* to be "settled law".

The ruling did not go down well. There was an uproar among American voters heard 'round the world, and the decision mobilized tens of millions, resulting in an unprecedented Democratic wave in the first midterms of the Biden presidency.

Prior to *Dobbs*, there was a considerable spectrum of regulation in place regarding pregnancy stage: in the *Roe* decision, the federal government retained the power to restrict abortion, and full bans were permitted after fetal viability, provided those bans allowed for threats to the mother's life.

Post-*Dobbs*, states were freed to decide for themselves. Ten of these – Alaska, Arizona, California, Florida, Kansas, Massachusetts, Minnesota, Montana, New Jersey, and New Mexico – protect the right to abortion via their state constitutions, protections that exceed the previous federal ones. Heavily conservative states – Kentucky, Indiana, Tennessee, West Virginia, Texas, Oklahoma, Missouri, Arkansas, Louisiana, Alabama, Mississippi, Idaho, and the Dakotas – have declared abortion illegal.

Voter backlash went beyond the 2022 midterms when, in April 2023, Janet Protasiewicz was elected to the Wisconsin Supreme Court, tipping its ideological balance to 4-3 for a reversal of the state's abortion restrictions. (She was also expected to impact the state's quest to end the use of gerrymandered legislative maps.) More than $40 million was spent on her election, making it the most expensive judicial election in US history.

State Republican lawmakers immediately moved to impeach her.

And in August, voters in conservative Ohio rallied to resist a Republican initiative to change the state's constitution to make it harder to amend, with a requirement of a 60% supermajority – a move that would allow minorities to prevail over majorities. The referendum to impose this requirement was a pushback against abortion activists intent on reversing the state's abortion ban, which made news when an Ohio woman, learning that her baby could not survive outside the womb, was denied abortion services and had to seek support in Michigan, which initially threw up barriers but eventually accommodated her.

Despite the state's red hue, the referendum was defeated 57.1% to 42.9%.

Subsequently, Ohio made the news again when a 10-year-old rape victim was forced by the state's "fetal heartbeat law" to travel to Indiana for an abortion.

As if that weren't enough, lawmakers in Texas are, at this writing, trying (in vain) to make it illegal for a pregnant woman in the state to travel to another state for an abortion.

When Amy Gardner told Josh "you don't screw around with that," it must have seemed inconceivable to every viewer watching that we would one day actually see *Roe* overturned. Yet here we are.

But we can take heart in the overwhelming backlash we've witnessed. We can reasonably conclude that the conservative forces pushing this cultural lever are shooting themselves in the foot, doing their cause more harm than good in the long run.

And, of course, we can feel great satisfaction in noting that *The West Wing* got it right, once again.

"I was wrong. I was. I was just — I was wrong! Come on, we know that. Lots of times, we don't know what right or wrong is, but lots of times we do and come on, this is one. I may not have had sinister intent at the outset. But there were plenty of opportunities for me to make it right. No one in government takes responsibility for anything anymore. We fluster, we obfuscate, rationalize. Everybody does it, that's what we say. So we come to occupy a moral safehouse where everyone's to blame so no one's guilty. I'm to blame. I was wrong."

~President Bartlet

The Wrath of the Whatever from High Atop the Thing

The Electoral College

It's Election Night. President Bartlet's contest against his Republican challenger, Florida Governor Rob Ritchie, will be decided soon.[44]

And in the Roosevelt Room, Toby mentions the two speeches he's written to CJ and Sam. CJ is surprised there are two speeches.

"I've got a speech if he wins, I've got a speech if he doesn't," Toby explains.

"You wrote a concession?" Sam is aghast.

"Of course I wrote a concession! You want to tempt the wrath of the whatever from high atop the thing?"

"No."

"Then go outside, turn around three times and spit! What the hell's the matter with you?"

"It's like 25 degrees outside!"

"Go!"

Josh walks in.

"He wrote a concession speech," Sam tattles.

"Of course he wrote a concession speech. Why wouldn't he? What possible reason would he have for not writing a concession speech?"

"The wrath from high atop the thing."

"He upped and said we were gonna-" Toby tattles back.

"No, you've got to go outside, turn around three times and curse."

"Spit."

"Spit and curse."

"Do everything. Go!"

---

44 In "Election Night", S4E7.

We'd actually seen Toby's superstitious nature with regard to voting before. It happened in "Six Meetings Before Lunch",[45] when the staff had gathered in the Mural Room during the Senate vote to confirm Supreme Court Justice Roberto Mendoza, and the bullpen staffers started popping champagne corks.

"Put it down! Put it down! Put it down!"

"Toby-"

"No champagne!"

"We're just getting ready to-"

"Put it down! Everyone in this room, let me have your attention, please! The law of our land mandates that Presidential appointees be confirmed by a majority of the Senate. A majority being half plus one for a total of what, Ginger?"

"Fifty-one."

"Fifty-one Yea votes is what we see on the screen before a drop of wine is swallowed! Because there's a little thing called what, Bonnie?"

"Tempting fate?"

"'Tempting fate' is what it's called! In the three months this man has been on my radar screen, I have aged 48 years. This is my day of jubilee, and I will not have it screwed up by what, Bonnie?"

"By tempting fate."

"By tempting fate!"

Toby's reticence to tempt fate, to avoid the wrath of the whatever from high atop the thing, is undoubtedly a byproduct of his win-loss record as a political operative – a city council race, two Congressional elections, a Senate race, a gubernatorial campaign, and a national campaign – all without a single victory.[46]

But we have even more reason to be wary of the wrath of the whatever, after our real-world presidential contest of 2000.

Vice-President Al Gore was neck-and-neck with Texas Governor George W. Bush, and on the morning after the election, Bush had

---

[45] S1E18.

[46] In "In the Shadow of Two Gunmen, Pt. I", S2E1.

acquired 246 electoral votes to Gore's 250. All that remained was Florida, where it was so close that a recount was undertaken. This would take more than a month. (On the night of the election, NBC, ABC, CBS, CNN and Fox all called the election for Gore.)

Bush was leading Gore as the night wore on and the count continued, but the margin was under 2,000. Bush's lead continued to dwindle, all the way down to just over 300 on the day after the election.

That margin was so slim that a recount was mandatory under state law. This included overseas ballots, 680 of which had been accepted but had arrived after the legal deadline or were unsigned/undated.

In December, the US Supreme Court ruled by a vote of 7-2 that the state Supreme Court's ruling requiring the recount was unconstitutional, reversing that ruling. The state Supreme Court was ordered to modify the original case, ending the recount, securing the original certified total, giving Bush the state and its 25 electoral votes.

The electoral total was then 271-266 – the slimmest possible. Gore won the popular vote by 543,895 votes with 50,999,897 – 48.4%.

That one hurt, of course, and led us into the most unjust war in US history (which is saying something) in Iraq. But far worse was the contest of 2016, which had greater consequences still.

It was inconceivable to almost everyone we don't today see as part of MAGA that Donald Trump would ever win the presidency; Trump himself was stunned when he learned he'd won.[47] And, in fact, his defeat the popular vote was profound: he lost by almost 3,000,000 votes.[48] Like Bush, however, he won the electoral college. Wisconsin, Michigan and Pennsylvania had all been forecast for Clinton, but Trump took all three. Trump took the latter at 1:35am EST, bumping him to 267 electoral votes – just three shy of a win. Half an hour later, the second congressional districts of Maine

---

[47] So certain was Trump that he would lose that he booked a small ballroom, rather than a large one, for what he assumed would be a concession speech: "I said if we're going to lose, I don't want a big ballroom."

[48] The vote was 65,853,514 (Clinton) - 63,984,82 (Trump).

and Nebraska came in, giving him two more. At 269, victory for Clinton became impossible.

And half an hour after that came the Wisconsin win, another 10 electoral votes, giving Trump a clear majority and making him president-elect.

Trump did not have to rely on an accommodating Supreme Court for his electoral win, though it's telling that his popular-vote loss was more than five times that of Bush's. It was the fifth presidential electoral win/popular vote loss in US history.

What's the lesson here? Toby's exactly right: *don't tempt the wrath of the whatever from high atop the thing!* Remember Yogi Berra's declaration that "It ain't over till it's over."

Toby, of course, did more than just prohibit premature champagne. He did what we all should do.

When Chief Justice Roy Ashland was hospitalized, Toby talks in his office with associate counsel Joe Quincy, recalling the time when he met Ashland:[49]

"I was a student at City College. Student organizing committee got him to give a speech about the history of voting rights. We were hanging from the rafters."

"I talked to him afterwards. I mean, he wouldn't remember me. But I spent the next six weeks organizing a voter registration drive."

And there's CJ, in the weeks before the re-elect, rallying for young voters in "College Kids":[50]

"Twenty-five years ago, half of all 18-to-24-year-olds voted. Today it's 25%. Eighteen-to-24-year-olds represent 33% of the population but only account for 7% of the voters. Think government isn't about you? How many of you have student loans to pay? How many have credit-card debt? How many want clean air and clean water and civil liberties? How many want jobs? How many want kids? How many want their kids to go to good schools and walk on

---

[49] In "Separation of Powers", S5E7.

[50] S4E3.

safe streets? Decisions are made by those who show up! You gotta rock the vote!"

"We're a team. From the President and Leo on through, we're a team... We win together, we lose together, we celebrate and we mourn together. And defeats are softened and victories sweetened because we did them together. And if you don't like this team, then, there's the door.

"It's great to be in the know. It's great to have the scoop, to have the skinny, to be able to go to a reporter and say, 'I know something you don't know.' And so the press becomes your constituents and you sell out the team... So, an item will appear in the paper tomorrow, and it'll be embarrassing to me and embarrassing to the President. I'm not gonna have a witch hunt. I'm not gonna huff and puff. I'm not gonna take anyone's head off. I'm simply gonna say this: you're my guys. And I'm yours... and there's nothing I wouldn't do for you."

~Toby

"Embarrass us like this, and we will give the same back to you tenfold!"

Political Retribution

Two seats have opened up on the Federal Election Commission at the same time, and President Bartlet has the idea that he can appoint to election reformers to those seats. This would mean the FEC might actually start getting something done in the area of election reform, but it's dicey territory: though the president has the authority to make those appointments, it has long been the peacekeeping tradition that the president appoint innocuous chairwarmers chosen by Senate leadership. Since the Senate is controlled by the Republicans during Bartlet's tenure, they will surely put up two completely empty candidates.

Bartlet decides to go for it, selecting two reformers. He is warned by his staff that this won't fly, and he realizes it's a long shot, but all the same he sends Josh to Senate leadership just to feel them out.[51]

"I came here as a courtesy, Jerry," Josh says in the meeting. "I came at the request of Leo McGarry. The President is strong considering John Branford Bacon and Patty Calhoun to fill in the two seats."

"I'm pretty sure we've already got our two guys, don't we?" replies Steve Onorato, chief of staff to the Senate Majority Leader. "Grant Kalen and Joe Barkley."

"Two people who oppose any campaign finance reform."

"Josh, look, we can't have this meeting every time the President wakes up in the morning and decides to make the world better. The party leadership's gonna choose a Republican. The party leadership's gonna choose a Democrat. That's the way it's always been. That's the way it's gonna be. That's the way it is."

"The President makes appointments to the Federal Election Commission," Josh says.

---

[51] In "Let Bartlet Be Bartlet", S1E19.

"And the Senate confirms them," Onorato fires back. "And I'm speaking for the majority leader. Embarrass us like this, and we will give the same back to you tenfold. Every piece of legislation the White House wants off the table will make a sudden appearance."

"Yeah. Steve's talking our greatest hits, Josh. 5-4-1, school prayer, Family Support Act, Entertainment Decency Act. English as the national language."

"Wouldn't it be easier to just not confirm our nominees?" Josh asks.

"Oh, we're gonna do that, too."

Josh is aghast.

"Are you saying that in addition to voting down our nominees, there's gonna be political retribution for having nominated them in the first place?"

"Yes. You know why? Because you know if you do this, you're gonna lose, and we're gonna look bad winning. I also got to say that I reject the suggestion that the best way to maintain free speech is by having government regulate it."

"You know, four hours ago, this was a fool's errand for me, and the President knew it. This was a test balloon. This was a 'just out of curiosity, let's see what would happen if' meeting, but you've managed to get me on board."

Josh leaves, and he's fired up.

Shortly thereafter, President Bartlet prepares to announce his FEC nominees. Onorato and the Senate Majority Leader are watching via television.[52]

"Tomorrow morning, we're going to begin to change the way elections are supervised in this country," President Bartlet tells the television audience.

"He's going to name two finance reformers to the FEC," Onorato tells his boss. "He's going to name – damn it!"

"I am proud to nominate John Branford Bacon and Patricia Calhoun to the Federal Election Commission!" Bartlet announces, to great applause.

---

[52] In "Mandatory Minimums", S1E20.

"Josh Lyman! Get him on the phone!" demands the senator. "I'm gonna reach down his throat and take out his lungs with an ice-cream scoop!"

In the hotel from which Bartlet is giving his television address, Sam predicts that Josh is about to get a phone call.

"Powerful guy," he warns.

Josh knows.

Donna brings Josh a cell phone.

"Hi, senator," he says without preamble, "Why don't you take your legislative agenda and shove it up your ass?"

It's a funny scene, but of course retribution is a discouraging reality of politics, and has been for centuries. Revenge, getting even, is a behavior that is all too human and all too toxic in political discourse.

As above, we are living in times that have become blinking neon exemplars of the realities of political life that *The West Wing* called out. So much of what the show brought to our attention has played out in outlandish caricature these many years on, in ways that would have seemed ludicrously improbable in the early 2000s. And all of that owes to an increasingly extremist GOP and its standard-bearer, ex-president Donald Trump.

The former president is not only obsessed with retribution (after an entire lifetime spent honing it); he boasts of his dedication to it and brandishes it at every opportunity, in hopes of intimidating anyone who might think about opposing him.

Incidents of political retribution seldom if ever bubbled up to the surface of the media in the past. That changed in the Clinton presidency, and has since become not only standard practice but routine public spectacle, to our collective detriment.

When presidents attack

Steve Onorato, in the scenes with Josh above, foreshadows US politics-to-come in an interesting way; he vows to Josh that if the president nominates his own preferred reformers to the FEC, the

GOP Congress will hit them back "tenfold". In this, he serves as herald to the most retributive politician in living memory: Donald Trump.

Trump's obsession with revenge and retribution has flared into a political pandemic since he entered politics, poisoning the party that claims him and weighing down any attempt at communication or cooperation that might stick its head out between the two major parties.

"If they screw you, screw them back *ten times as hard*," he said in a speech to the National Achievers Congress in Sydney, Australia in 2011 (though he's said it countless times since). His wife Melania reminded us all during his term as president, saying, "As you may know by now, when you attack him, he will punch back *ten times harder*."

At the time, we might remember a pundit or two playing that quote out: if one child hits another on the playground, and the second child hits back, that's to be expected, and we simply separate the two; but if the second child leaps onto the first and pummels him with ten hard blows, that's something else entirely. That's not self-defense; that's brutality.

Trump unapologetically deploys this philosophy at every opportunity, with all its mindless macho, out of a conviction that the world finds it intimidating. There are countless exemplars from his brief White House tenure alone:

- The state of New York has investigated Trump's businesses, fining him and his children for tax fraud; the state has also indicted him for campaign finance violations over his hush money payments to Stormy Daniels. In retaliation, Trump punished New York by declaring it ineligible for the Global Entry program;
- Trump called for the return of $3.5 billion in federal funds allocated to California for the development of its high-speed rail project after the state sued over his emergency declaration to pay for his US-Mexico wall;
- Trump did everything in his power to unravel the legacy of his predecessor, Barack Obama, most famously attempting to repeal the Affordable Care Act – which

would have rendered 54 million Americans effectively uninsurable;
- Not restricting his retribution to Americans, Trump withheld $300 million in funds from the United Nations Relief and Works Agency for Palestine Refugees to punish Palestinian leadership for opposing his recognition of Jerusalem as Israel's capital; the decision reduced the UNRWA budget by over 80 percent and put the lives of millions of refugees in jeopardy.

Over two years after vacating the Oval Office, Trump had, if anything, gotten much worse. In the aftermath of the Jan. 6, 2021 assault on Congress, and under the clouds of multiple indictments for his role in the attack, as well as his theft of classified documents and conspiracy to overturn the 2020 presidential election, Trump went 24/7 retributive.

After declaring his candidacy for the 2024 Republican nomination, he told his MAGA faithful, "In 2016, I declared, 'I am your voice.' Today, I add: I am your warrior, I am your justice, and for those of you who have been wronged and betrayed, I am your retribution!"

After his indictments in special prosecutor Jack Smith's investigations, he lit up on his Truth Social network with a post declaring, "IF YOU GO AFTER ME, I'M COMING AFTER YOU!"

In a 2023 interview with Glenn Beck, he said he'd have "no choice" but to lock up his political opponents if he wins the White House in 2024.

Hours after pleading "not guilty" in one of the Smith indictments, Trump met with reporters and declared that if he wins, "I will appoint a real special prosecutor to go after the most corrupt president in the history of America, Joe Biden, and go after the Biden crime family."

Party-to-party

And this toxic attitude has now permeated the Republican Congress, which has sought to remove Fulton County District Attorney Fani Willis for indicting Trump and 19 others for their attempt to overturn Georgia's 2020 vote.

And other Republicans are following their party leader's example. Florida Gov. Ron DeSantis, out-maneuvered by Disney in their pushback against his anti-LGBTQ crusade, has stepped up his attacks, even going after the Mouse for the discounts it gives its employees.

"There clearly was retribution politically against them," conceded even former MAGA footsoldier Mike Pence.

We want to believe it couldn't get any uglier.

A proportional response

To Sorkin's credit, he gave us a bit of retributive thunder in Jed Bartlet in *The West Wing*'s earliest days, only to have our favorite president learn his lesson right away.

His physician, Capt. Morris Tolliver, gives him his weekly check-up and throws in a flu shot. They banter, which Bartlet clearly enjoys; Leo tells Morris aside that "he likes you, Morris. He feels better after he's talked to you. I think there have been days when you've lightened the load a little." Tolliver informs Bartlet that he'll be missing a week, as he's flying to the Middle East to do some teaching.[53]

The Air Force transport carrying Tolliver and others to a teaching hospital in Amman is blown out of the sky by the Syrian defense ministry. Stunned and furious, Bartlet vows to Leo that "I'm gonna blow them off the face of the earth with the fury of God's own thunder" - words Leo finds disturbing.

In the Situation Room, Admiral Fitzwallace presents him with three proportional response scenarios – retaliations that are sized to

---

[53] In "Post Hoc, Ergo Proctor Hoc", S1E2.

match Syria's attack. Bartlet is not impressed; he orders Fitzwallace to put together a Trump option – to punch back ten times as hard.

"What is the virtue of a proportional response?" he begins by asking.[54]

"It isn't virtuous, Mr. President. It's all there is, sir."

"It is not all there is."

"Pardon me, Mr. President, just what else is there?"

"A *dis*-proportional response! Let the word ring forth from this time and this place, you kill an American, any American, we don't come back with a proportional response, we come back with total disaster!"

"Are you suggesting we carpet-bomb Damascus?" asks a general.

"General, I am suggesting that you and Admiral Fitzwallace and Secretary Hutchinson and the rest of the national security team take the next sixty minutes and put together a US response scenario that doesn't make me think we are just docking somebody's damn allowance!"

When the president returns, Fitzwallace offers a brilliant response:

"Mr. President, we put together a scenario by which we attack Hassan airport. It's three main terminals and two runways. In addition to the civilian causalities, which could register in the thousands, the strike would temporally cripple the region's ability to receive medical supplies and bottled water. I think Mr. Cashman and Secretary Hutchinson would each tell you what I'm sure you already know, sir: that this strike would be seen at home and abroad as a staggering overreaction by a first time Commander-in-Chief. That without the support of our allies, without a Western Coalition, without Great Britain and Japan and without Congress, you'll have doled out a five-thousand-dollar punishment for a fifty-buck crime, sir.

"Mr. President, the proportional response doesn't empty the options box for the future, the way an all-out assault-"

---

[54] In "A Proportional Response", S1E3.

Bartlet stops him, getting the point, and orders Fitzwallace to carry out the proportional response.

Bartlet's motivation for retribution here is, of course, as righteous as Trump's motivations are petty; but the point remains, and is poignantly made.

The Josh Lyman Doctrine

What do we make of all this? Our first thought might be one of dread; now that we've arrived in this terrible era of winner-take-all politics – an era that was beginning to take shape even while *The West Wing* was still on the air – are we here to stay? Now that the genie's out of the bottle, and we've seen an entire US party given over to the politics of intimidation and vengeance, is there any hope that civility and decency will ever be restored?

Arguments can be made both ways, as the new face of the Republican Party, made over in Trump's image, is not winning any new converts; on the other hand, we've seen breathtaking authoritarian impulses emerge in countless GOP politicians, and wonder if it's possible to contain them all.

But one thing is certain: the correct response is not to kowtow or submit; refusing to do so may fan an already-terrifying flame, but bowing will only embolden and encourage them.

Josh, we can agree, had the right idea, and Disney (among others) is following his lead: when they come at you and threaten you with retribution and revenge, when they try to intimidate you and pressure you and shout you down, the correct response is to take a deep breath and say,

Shove it up your ass!

"I'd feel better if it meant just once I could go to a doctor without filling out something on a clipboard."

Healthcare

The Family Wellness Act, an omnibus health bill sponsored by the Oval Office, is about to be voted on by the Senate. Its $6 billion in apportionments for illnesses and conditions that affect children has been shepherded to fruition by Josh, a great victory for the Bartlet presidency...[55]

...until a cantankerous old senator named Howard Stackhouse unexpectedly filibusters, refusing to let the bill come to the Senate until Josh adds a rider directing $57 million to a child autism program Stackhouse wants. The filibuster threatens to torpedo the entire bill – until Donna realizes that Stackhouse is taking this stand because he himself has an autistic grandson.[56]

Matt Santos, running against Republican Sen. Arnold Vinick to inherit Bartlet's office, takes up the banner when the two debate on live television, presenting a plan to move toward universal healthcare by opening Medicare up for everyone – a plan his GOP opponent vigorously opposes.[57]

This commitment to quality healthcare for all as a national priority is in line with liberal/progressive ideology across the board: healthcare should be universal, affordable, easily accessible, and of the highest quality. We've seen this vision, and the competing

---

[55] In "The Stackhouse Filibuster", S2E17.

[56] The scene when help finally arrives in the Senate chamber, and Stackhouse finds himself supported by his fellow senators (and, behind the scenes, the president and his staff) is one of *The West Wing*'s greatest stand-up-and-cheer moments.

[57] In "The Debate", S7E7.

conservative vision, battling it out for decades now. It's gotten right up in our faces; and though Sorkin and his successors could have no sense of it at the time, the whole thing erupted into the showdown of the century not long after *The West Wing* left the airwaves – with Obamacare.

Some US healthcare history

First, a little history: the struggle over government's role in the personal health of the nation's citizens has existed as long as modern medicine has been around. The two positions mentioned above, and all the variations in between, have never left the arena of public debate.

Theodore Roosevelt was the first president to endorse a public insurance program, as the National Convention of Insurance Commissioners rolled out a plan for state adoption. Not long after, the American Association for Labor Legislation began to press for compulsory health insurance. Soon, at the university level, programs insuring teachers appeared, foreshadowing what would become Blue Cross.

Business joined in as a matter of necessity during the Great Depression, with many executives authorizing coverage for workers. On the government side, the Federal Security Agency appeared in 1939, eventually evolving into the Department of Health and Human Services. The Social Security Board then recommended that national health insurance be added to the Social Security system. President Harry Truman, not long after assuming office, became the first president to propose universal healthcare.

Truman's successor, Dwight Eisenhower, proposed a federal reinsurance program to expand access to private insurance, and implemented health insurance for military families.

Then came the Medicare system under Lyndon Johnson – the foundation of what we have today. It was vigorously opposed by the American Medical Association; "socialized medicine" became a conservative scare term. But Medicare prevailed, within the limitations set at its initiation.

Richard Nixon reorganized prepaid group health care programs into what we now know as HMOs – health maintenance organizations – and legislation creates a federal certification program for them. Nixon followed up with his own proposal for a national health insurance program – rejected, ironically, by liberals and unions.

Jimmy Carter took up the problem, proposing an incremental approach that would phase in health care expansions gradually, allowing the federal budget to absorb them over time. He was vigorously opposed by Ted Kennedy, who favored a Big Bang approach that would introduce legislation calling for sweeping change and full implementation, budget be damned. His refusal to support Carter's more measured, sober approach was a prelude to challenging him for the nomination in 1980, and he wanted the healthcare win for himself. In so doing, he forced America to wait another 30 years for the healthcare access that Carter's plan would have provided.

In the following years, the hospital system in the US began to integrate as the privatization of healthcare rolled forward. Not surprisingly, healthcare costs during this period rose at twice the rate of inflation. In the Nineties, Congress once again failed to pass reform legislation.

And as the century ended, healthcare costs continued to climb; HMOs became increasingly powerful, with healthcare decisions being handed down to consumers not by doctors but by insurance staff; arriving in the new millennium, it was the norm that a serious illness could wipe a family out financially, costing them their home and savings and future.

...which brings us to Obamacare. Signed into law by President Barack Obama in 2010, the Affordable Care Act opened up access to health insurance to Americans with preexisting conditions – a monumental step forward – while dramatically reducing the number of uninsured and expanding access overall (increasing the number of Americans insured by 12 million). Republican legislators immediately began attacking it (see "Political Brinkmanship", above) and President Trump vowed to roll it back (mercifully, he failed utterly).

In the here-and-now, the Santos push for Medicare-for-All continues through Sen. Bernie Sanders, who in May 2023 said, "The current healthcare system in the United States is totally broken. It is totally dysfunctional, and it is extremely cruel." This was a prelude to his introduction of the Medicare for All Act of 2023, along with 112 Democratic co-sponsors.

At the time of this bill's introduction, according to a KFF analysis, about 23 million people are in medical debt, with 11 million owing more than $2,000 and 3 million owing more than $10,000.

"It is long overdue for us to end the international embarrassment of the United States being the only major country on earth that does not guarantee health care to all of its people," Sanders said. "Now is the time for a Medicare for All single-payer program."

Thom Hartmann's take: the decline in US healthcare owes much to the growing inequality in the nation from the Eighties onward. He noted a study by Richard Wilkinson and Kate Pickett that surveyed countries in the developed world, discovering that increases in inequality are directly related to declining outcomes across the board, including

- Infant mortality
- Life expectancy
- Depression
- Mental illness
- Teen pregnancy
- Obesity
- Educational performance in children
- Hypertension
- Heart disease
- Suicide
- Homicide

Per Hartmann, then, to address inequality is to address declining health outcomes.

He also noted that the consequences of Medicare-for-All are easily quantified:

- Private insurance companies would greatly shrink in number, catering only to the uber-wealthy;
- Big Pharma, which currently charges Americans far more for medicine than citizens of other countries pay, would be forced back into a more competitive posture, reducing stockholder dividends; development of new drugs would likely not be heavily impacted, as much of that research is government-funded anyway and other countries contribute to that enterprise;
- Doctors, as a profession, would make less money overall;
- Hospital networks would see big savings through the implementation of efficiencies that single-payer systems would bring; on the other hand, they would lose the ability to overbill
- A few dozen CEOs would have to retire and make due with the hundreds of millions they've already accumulated.

Battling Big Pharma

The reigning in of Big Pharma that would follow from a Medicare-for-All expansion addresses one of the biggest problems in the system, and one that *The West Wing* addressed more than once:

Forrest Sawyer is moderating the televised Santos-Vinick debate,[58] and asks Vinick:

"Senator, let me ask you about a related issue which is prescription drug prices and those prices have been going up at a rate more than double the inflation rate. So, would you favor re-importing American drugs from Canada where they are much cheaper?"

"You know why drugs are cheaper in Canada?" Vinick replies. "Because the government controls the price. Do you know how

---

[58] Ibid.

many life-saving drugs are invented in Canada? None, because the government controls the price."

"Well, Canadian laboratories have helped to create some very important drugs," Santos interjects.

"No, nothing like the miraculous drugs that the American pharmaceutical industry has given to the world," Vinick counters.

"*Given* to the world? I guess you haven't seen the price list lately, sir."

"Not long ago, if you were HIV positive in this country you were marked for death. Not anymore," Vinick says. "And that's thanks to our pharmaceutical companies. You know, in the 1970s, the most common cause for surgery was ulcers. Now, you get an ulcer, you take a pill. Is it an expensive pill? Yes. A dollar does seem like a lot to pay for one pill. But how does a dollar a day sound compared to a $30,000 surgery bill? So, are prescription drugs expensive? Yes. Do they save us from getting hit with much more expensive hospital bills? Yes. Do they save lives? Yes. American pharmaceutical companies save us money and they save lives and the Democrats can't stop attacking them."

"Why should the pharmaceutical companies get protection that no other American industry gets? We can buy anything else from Canada; why not prescription drugs?"

"Because the Canadian price controls are unfair to American companies."

"They're unfair?"

"Yes, they are."

"Well, is it unfair that AIDS victims have been dying for Africa for years because the drug companies are protecting their profit margins?"

"Drug-makers have lowered their prices in Africa dramatically."

"Yes, only after we have pushed them to do it and they are still not low enough to reach everyone who really needs them in Africa."

And that, too, was a *West Wing* moment, in "In This White House":

"How can you tell us this isn't about profit maximization?" asks President Nimbala of the Republic of Equatorial Kundo through his translator, to Big Pharma executives in the Roosevelt Room. "Why do you sell Amprex for half the price in Norway than you do in my country?"

"I don't think that's the issue," one executive replies.

"Let's make it the issue," Toby interjects.

"You can't compare prices worldwide, Toby."

"I am the one who asked you the question," President Nimbala says. "I'd appreciate it if you directed your answer to me."

"President Nimbala. When you sell to small pharmacies, as we do in Norway, a different price is set."

"Norway, ten dollars per unit US; my country, twenty-three dollars per unit US."

"Retail mark-up, taxes, pharmacy discounts... these things vary widely," the executive replies.

"What are your annual sales of Fluconazole alone? A billion dollars."

"I don't understand your point, sir."

"I think President Nimbala's saying that there's more money in giving a white guy an erection than curing a black guy of AIDS."

Big Pharma's stranglehold on this corner of the healthcare market has oscillated far out of control over the past 40 years, selling its product at prices often far out of reach of those who need them most. This, combined with HMOs having a say over which drugs they will or won't pay for, puts many Americans in a hopeless position. The bulwark of lobbyists who have kept reform legislation at bay has held for many years; but recent efforts by President Joe Biden to reverse the economic models of the past 40 years have yielded success in this domain, specifically.

Historian Heather Cox Richardson, made several important points about Biden's accomplishment in a blog post on August 29, 2023:

> "For far too long, Americans have paid more for prescription drugs than any major economy. And while the pharmaceutical industry makes record profits, millions of Americans are forced to choose between paying for medications they need to live or paying for food, rent, and other basic necessities. Those days are ending," President Joe Biden declared today.

The government announced the first ten drugs whose prices it will negotiate with pharmaceutical companies for about 65 million Medicare recipients. Until now, the United States has been virtually alone as the only country in which the government did not negotiate or regulate medicine prices, instead allowing companies to set whatever prices they believe the market will bear. Since their products often are the difference between life and death, it turns out the market will bear quite high prices, but - as Biden observed - those prices often force consumers to sacrifice in other ways to afford them.

A 2021 study by the RAND corporation found that drug prices average 2.56 times higher in the US than in 32 other countries. For name brand drugs, US prices were 3.44 times those in comparable nations.

As Amy Goldstein and Daniel Gilbert explained today in the *Washington Post*, when Congress created Medicare and Medicaid in 1965 as part of President Lyndon B. Johnson's Great Society program, it covered drugs administered in a health care setting but excluded those a patient took at home. In 2003, after almost 40 years of medical innovation had significantly changed our management of chronic illnesses, Congress included those drugs under a separate Medicare plan—Part D—or as part of managed-care plans, but to get Republicans behind the bill, Congress explicitly prohibited the government from negotiating the prices of medications.

In 2021 a nearly three-year investigation by the House Committee on Oversight and Reform, then overseen by Democrats as they held the majority in the House of Representatives, concluded that "[d]rug companies have raised prices relentlessly for decades while manipulating the patent system and other laws to delay competition from lower-priced generics. These companies have specifically targeted the US market for higher prices, even while cutting prices in other countries, because weaknesses in our health care system have allowed them to get away with outrageous prices and anticompetitive conduct."

Republicans sided with the drug company executives who insisted that high prices were necessary to create an incentive for drug companies to innovate, as their investment in research and development depends on the revenue they expect from new drugs. But the committee's report said their investigation concluded that "sky-high drug prices are not justified by the need to innovate. The largest drug companies spend more on payouts for investors and executives than on research and development. And many blockbuster drugs rely on scientific discoveries from research funded by taxpayers, while drug companies' R&D spending often focuses on minor changes to extend patent protection and block lower-priced competitors."

In 2022, Democrats passed the Inflation Reduction Act without a single Republican vote. That law permits the government to negotiate with pharmaceutical companies over drug prices the government will pay.

The ten drugs listed in today's announcement are among those with the highest total spending in Medicare Part D, and today the Department of Health and Human Services released a report that 9 million seniors paid a total of $3.4 billion for these drugs in 2022. The Congressional Budget Office, the nonpartisan agency that provides budget and economic information to Congress, estimates that government negotiation over these drugs will save taxpayers about $98.5 billion over ten years. If a drug maker refuses to negotiate, it either will face a significant tax or must withdraw from Medicare and Medicaid.

This measure is extraordinarily popular. More than eighty percent of Americans want the government to be able to negotiate drug costs...

We're not there yet. But we're getting there.

"You know, I have no position on capital punishment. I try to get worked up about it, it seems like I should. But the truth is, I honestly don't care if Simon Cruz lives or dies. And I suppose if it brings some measure of comfort to the families of the victims, then why the hell not?

"Except... at 12:04, that's when the warden calls me. That's my job tonight. I have to go in and tell the President that Simon Cruz is dead and we're the ones who killed him. So... I just wish I didn't know his mother's name was Sophia, is all I'm saying."

~CJ

"The streets of Heaven are too crowded with angels tonight!"

Terrorism

The West Wing didn't shy away from the subject of terrorism, even though it was a traumatic topic for the nation as a whole from the third season on. Most prominently, the story arc of Qumari Defense Minister Abdul Shareef,[59] who is secretly a Bahji terrorist leader, and his plot to bring down the Golden Gate Bridge (a storyline that swung uncomfortably close to the real-world collapse of the World Trade Center).

In the wake of 9/11, that's where the thoughts of most Americans went when they heard the word *terrorism* – attack from without. That's natural, as we'd just been attacked more savagely from without than ever before, at a cost of 2,977 American lives.

But most acts of terrorism in the US, before then and since, have actually been acts of domestic terrorism – perpetrated on Americans, by Americans.

It's important at this point, having already covered mass shootings above, to make note of Secret Service lead Ron Butterfield's definition of terrorism:[60]

"Muslim extremists don't get personal. They don't know your name, they don't care. They don't want one person, they want dozens or hundreds, that's why they don't use bullets. Killing one person is a waste of a bomb. He wants you, why doesn't he want me?"

One such bomb went off at Kennison State University in "20 Hours in America, Pt. II",[61] killing dozens of college students and staff.

---

[59] In the third season episodes 19-21.

[60] In "Enemies Foreign and Domestic", S3E18.

[61] S4E2.

"More than any time in recent history, America's destiny is not of our own choosing," President Bartlet said shortly thereafter. "We did not seek, nor did we provoke an assault on our freedom and our way of life. We did not expect, nor did we invite a confrontation with evil. Yet the true measure of a people's strength is how they rise to master that moment when it does arrive. Forty-four people were killed a couple of hours ago at Kennison State University. Three swimmers from the men's team were killed and two others are in critical condition. When, after having heard the explosion from their practice facility, they ran into the fire to help get people out. Ran *into* the fire.

"The streets of heaven are too crowded with angels tonight. They're our students and our teachers and our parents and our friends. The streets of heaven are too crowded with angels, but every time we think we have measured our capacity to meet a challenge, we look up and we're reminded that that capacity may well be limitless. this is a time for American heroes."

The September 11 attacks aside, we've experienced very little foreign terrorism on US soil. Far right-wing extremist groups have outperformed radical Islamic extremists 3-to-1 since 9/11, according to a 2017 report by the US Government Accountability Office.

We've seen all too much domestic terrorism.

Before *The West Wing*:

- there was the 16th Street Baptist Church Bombing of 1963, in which 19 sticks of dynamite planted by KKK members killed four young black girls;
- the Oklahoma City Bombing of 1995, in which Timothy McVeigh and Terry Nichols blew up the Alfred P. Murrah Federal Building, killing 168 and injuring 680;
- the Centennial Olympic Park Bombing of 1996, in Atlanta, where a right-wing terrorist disrupted the Summer Olympics disrupted the Summer Olympics with a pipe bomb, killing 2 and injuring 111.

…among many others. Following 9/11,

- the 2012 Aurora, Colorado cinema shooting, in which a lone shooter dressed in tactical gear threw gas grenades, then opened fire on theatergoers, killing 12 and injuring 70;
- the Boston Marathon Bombing in 2013,[62] in which two brothers planted two pressure-cooker bombs, killing 3 and injuring 281 (including 17 lost limbs);
- the Charlottesville car attack in 2017, in which a white supremacist drove his car into a crowd of counter-protesters, killing 1 and injuring 35.

All random, all violent - and all white.

All the shootings mentioned above in the chapter on gun control are additional examples of domestic terrorism – violence carried out not against one, but many, randomly, as acts of protest or chaos. They speak to a societal epidemic – one that is spreading, rather than receding.

We can note with interest that the vast majority of these domestic terror events were carried out with guns, rather than bombs. The bomb, as Ron Butterfield points out to CJ, is the preferred weapon of the terrorist. Get control of guns, and domestic terror incidents will drop dramatically, we can reasonably assume.

We can also take note of Sam Seaborn's observations on terrorism, pointing out to a group of students in the White House mess during a lockdown "it has a 100% failure rate. Not only do terrorists always fail at what they're after, they pretty much always succeed in strengthening whatever it is they're against."[63]

"What about the IRA?" asks one young man.

"The Brits are still there. The Protestants are still there. Basque extremists have been staging terrorist attacks in Spain for decades with no result. Left Wing Red Brigades from the Sixties and Seventies, from the Bader-Meinhoff gang in Germany to the

---

[62] Revisited in an episode of Sorkin's subsequent HBO series, *The Newsroom*.

[63] In "Isaac and Ishmael", the Season 3 special episode.

Weatherman in the US have tried to take over capitalism. You tell me. How's capitalism doing?"

"Yeah, but weren't we terrorists at the Boston Tea Party?" asks a young woman.

"Nobody got hurt at the Boston Tea Party," Sam replies. "The only people that got hurt was some fancy boys who didn't have anything to wash down their crumpets with. We jumped out from behind bushes, while the British came down the road in their bright red jackets, but never has a war been so courteously declared. It was on parchment with calligraphy and 'Your highness, we beseech you on this day in Philadelphia to bite me, if you please.'"

Get control of the guns, certainly, and beyond that, take a page from Sam: understand that terrorism accomplishes nothing, and its perpetrators never last. There may be no way to end it altogether, but we can reduce its incidence by lowering the temperature in issues of race, religion, and political differences, wherever they might be found – pushing back against the *causes* of terrorism, first and foremost.

And let's not forget that the domestic terrorism we see most happens in our schools, and its victims are our children.

The streets of Heaven are, at this point, far too crowded.

"Omigod, you're putting my mother's cats on the Supreme Court!"

The Balance of the Court

Justice Owen Brady has died, leaving President Bartlet another opportunity to fill a Supreme Court seat. His problem is that, unlike the Mendoza appointment, where he was replacing one liberal justice with another, Brady was a staunch conservative; if he tries to fill Brady's seat with another liberal, he can count on the Senate to shut him down.[64]

At the very least, he wants to appoint a moderate, and he and the staff reason that if they have highly-visible chats with ultra-liberal justices and then name their moderate nominee, the process might be much less painless. Josh and Toby, then, begin taking meetings with jurists sure to terrify the Senate right.

One of these is Evelyn Baker Lang (see above), for whom Josh falls head over heels. She is *exactly* what the court needs, in his mind, given the deteriorating condition of Chief Justice Roy Ashland (see above) - a 'liberal lion', just like Ashland. But he knows (and Toby reminds him) that the Senate will never, ever confirm her. They are even more certain of this when she reveals to them that she had an abortion while in law school.

On the other hand, she's the perfect chill: the very sight of her in the White House will frighten the Republican Senate so much that they'll hold the door for their moderate nominee, the competent but conviction-free Brad Shelton.

But Josh can't stomach the idea of another moderate on the high court. "If we had a bench full of moderates in '54," he tells Toby, "'Separate but Equal would still be on the books and this place would still have two sets of drinking fountains."

---

[64] In "The Supremes", S5E17.

Donna's mom sends a batch of cookies with a picture of her two cats taped to the tin. She explains that when her parents' cat died, they went out to get a new one and couldn't agree on a cat, so they each picked one.

Josh gets an idea: convince the president to nominate Lang for the ailing Ashland, and let the Judiciary Committee pick any conservative Republican they please.

"Two voices articulating the debate at either end of the spectrum," he argues to the president. Bartlet tells them to see if Ashland will step down, if Lang were to be his replacement.

They take it to Ashland, who loves the idea and readily agrees. Afterwards, Bartlet meets with Lang, then the Republican candidate Christopher Mulready, a fire-breathing right-winger:

"Who's at the top of the list?" Mulready asks, when he and Bartlet are alone in the Oval Office.

"Brad Shelton."

"Really?"

"You don't like him?"

"He's a fine jurist. And in the event that Charmine, Lafayette, Hoyt, Clarke and Brandegen all drop dead this summer, the center will still be well-tended."[65]

"You want another Brady?"

"Sure, just like you'd like another Ashland - who wouldn't? The court was at its best when Brady was fighting Ashland."

"Plenty of good law written by the voice of moderation."

"Who writes the extraordinary dissent?" Mulready asks. "The one-man minority opinion whose time hasn't come but 20 years later some circuit court clerk digs it up at 3 in the morning? Brennan railing against censorship. Harlan's jeremiad against Jim Crowe."

"Maybe you some day?"

"They can't put me on the court, just like you can't put Evelyn Lang on the court. It's Sheltons from here on in."

---

[65] We're left wondering where Roberto Mendoza went. Or, for that matter, Justice Dreifort, mentioned by White House Council Lionel Tribbey in "And It's Surely to Their Credit" (S2E5).

"There are 4,000 protestors outside this building worried about who's going to land in that seat. We can't afford to alienate all of them."

"We all have our roles to play, sir. Yours is to nominate someone who doesn't alienate people."

But Bartlet goes for it, putting Mulready in Brady's chair and naming Lang as the first female Chief Justice of the Supreme Court.

On the other hand...

Twenty years later, there has been considerable Supreme Court turnover – and Donald Trump appointed three ultra-conservative justices, leaving the public *screaming* for a balanced court – or, at the very least, some moderation.

Neil Gorsuch, confirmed in April of 2017, replaced the conservative originalist Antonin Scalia. His confirmation vote was 54-45. His appointment was highly controversial, as Scalia had died a year earlier, and Barack Obama – who had the constitutional duty to appoint his successor (he put up Merrick Garland) – was denied that duty by Senate Majority Leader Mitch McConnell. McConnell's justification was that Obama had no business appointing a Supreme Court justice in the final year of his administration.

Brett Kavanaugh, Trump's second installation, took his post on October 6, 2018, amid much controversy: in addition to a history as an undisciplined frat boy, he was under the cloud of sexual assault accusations. Moreover, he lost his temper during his confirmation hearings, in which he was confronted by one of his accusers, Christine Blasey Ford.[66] Kavanaugh replaced Anthony Kennedy, who unexpectedly retired.

---

[66] "But another kind of credibility was also at stake for Kavanaugh - that of a judge, whose legitimacy depends on our perception of him as rational, fair, calm, and nonpartisan. In this respect, the juxtaposition of Ford and of Kavanaugh was striking. It was Ford, by far, who had the more judicial demeanor. Kavanaugh often appeared to be having a petulant and distracted teen-age meltdown, interrupting the Democratic senators and rarely attempting to answer their questions directly. Ford appeared nervous but thoughtful, and earnestly focused on doing her best to 'be helpful,' as she put it at one point. His shouting filled the chamber, while she had to lean into a microphone to be heard. The even-tempered and dignified judicial persona that Kavanaugh has worked so hard to cultivate fell away to reveal

Finally, in the final months of the Trump Administration, Ruth Bader Ginsberg – truly a 'liberal lion' in the Roy Ashland sense - died after a long illness on September 18, 2022, clearing the path for Trump to name yet another justice. That new justice was Amy Coney Barrett, a favorite of the Christian Right and social conservatives. She was speedily confirmed, taking office barely a month after Ginsberg's death. In a stunning display of naked hypocrisy, Mitch McConnell – who had held up the nomination of Merrick Garland for a year, to keep a Supreme Court seat open for a Republican president to name – suddenly reversed his position that a president had no business naming a justice in his final year (Trump nominated Barrett a month before the 2020 election).

Gorsuch for Scalia was business-as-usual: conservative justice for conservative justice.

Kavanaugh for Kennedy, not so much; Kavanaugh was clearly more conservative than Kennedy, though Kennedy was the real-life version of Bartlet candidate Brad Shelton – not easily ideologically pigeon-holed, no great partisan convictions.

Barrett for Ginsberg was a travesty – a conservative originalist replacing a progressive civil rights, voting rights firebrand. This was exactly the sort of appointment that *The West Wing* was lamenting.

With Scalia/Kennedy/Ginsberg, there was balance; a far-right conservative, a swing vote, a far-left liberal. With Trump's trio – Gorsuch, Kavanaugh, Barrett – we have nothing but hard-core conservatives, and a very out-of-balance 6-3 court.

This trinity enabled the long-dreaded overturning of *Roe v. Wade* (see above), and has also weakened affirmative action with *Students for Fair Admissions v. President and Fellows of Harvard College* and *Students for Fair Admissions, v. University of North Carolina* in June 2023. That same month, the court annulled President Biden's

---

a sneering and volatile boy with his arms crossed, furious not to be getting his way.

"If there is a red flag here, it is not only Kavanaugh's failure to maintain composure during a tense and extraordinary hearing. It is, rather, the risk that the process itself, which Democrats and Republicans seem to agree has been a disaster, has been so damaging to Kavanaugh's psyche that partisan bitterness and rage will shape his temperament and his orientation to judicial work for a lifetime." - Jeannie Suk Gerson in *The New Yorker*, Sept. 28, 2018.

student loan debt forgiveness in *Biden v. Nebraska*, and struck a blow to LGBTQ rights by upholding a Christian web designer's right to refuse services to a gay couple in 303 Creative LLC v. Elenis – despite the fact that the plaintiff possessed no wedding website service and no gay couple had commissioned such a website, leading to the activist accusation that the court's ruling was "a license to discriminate."

In all of these cases, the vote was 6-3, with the conservatives voting as a block (the exception being the first, in which Justice Ketanji Brown Jackson (whom President Biden appointed) recused herself.

So, yes, an out-of-balance court is a serious concern.

The primary remedy for this imbalance has been an effort to expand the court from 9 seats to 13, per the Judiciary Act of 2023, sponsored by Representatives Hank Johnson, Edward Markey, Tina Smith, Adam Schiff, and Cori Bush. If such an expansion were to take place, it would be the seventh shift in the size of the high court in its history.

"At a time when the American people's confidence in the nation's highest court has fallen to a record low and Congressional Republicans have already employed their far-right judicial playbook by disregarding norms and precedent in the confirmations process, Congress must take action by once again expanding the Court," read the press release.[67]

The challenge to the legitimacy of the current Roberts Court has been exacerbated by issues of questionable ethical behavior on the part of Justice Clarence Thomas, on top of the revisiting of McConnell's open stacking of the court.

"When a bully steals your lunch money in the schoolyard, you have to do something about it, or else the bully will come back over and over again," said Edward Markey. "So we're in this fight, and we're going to reclaim these seats. We're not going to allow the bully to win."

---

[67] Per a University of Chicago study, public confidence in the high court fell to 18% in 2023 – the lowest in half a century.

"This is not a conservative court, not in a legal sense," said Adam Schiff. "A conservative court would have some respect for precedent. This is instead a political and partisan court with a reactionary social agenda and the only question, Mitch McConnell having packed the court, is will we do anything about it or will we subject an entire generation of Americans to the loss of their rights?

"Dirtier air and dirtier water and dirtier elections? Is that the fate we would have for the next generation? My kids are both in their early 20 and I am not satisfied that they should have to live under a reactionary supreme court for their entire adult lives and I don't want anyone else's kids to have to suffer that fate."

Adding four seats to the existing nine could potentially shift the balance back in favor of the left to 7-6, if four liberal justices were appointed; but to attempt such a stacked appointment would undoubtedly cause the GOP to burn Washington to the ground. Even if such legislation name it through the House – unlikely – it would require President Biden to do as President Bartlet almost did, putting up Brad Sheltons, rather than liberal lions.

So *The West Wing* called it wrong, with "It's Sheltons, from here on is." Clearly the GOP will eschew moderation at every turn when they have the power to impose their will. And while we can argue that the high court needs its liberal lions – of course it does, they're the ones who move society forward – we can also agree with Josh that balance is everything.

Because now we see all too clearly what happens when balance is missing.

"How can you be a member of this party??? This party who says that who you are is against the law?"

LGBTQ+

While Toby, Sam and CJ accompany President Bartlet to Portland on Air Force One, Josh remains behind at the White House, taking an evening meeting with Republican Congressman Matt Skinner, who is also a personal friend. Their topic is the Marriage Recognition Act, a controversial bill written by conservative Republicans to restrict the definition and benefits of marriage at the federal level – a bill, in other words, to deny gay persons access to legal marriage.[68]

"Josh, all the Marriage Recognition Act does is ensure that a radical social agenda isn't thrust upon an entire country that isn't ready for it yet."

"Thirty-two States have passed laws banning same-sex marriage. The States are doing a fine job protecting themselves from a radical social agenda without a federal shield... I like you guys who want to reduce the size of government and make it just small enough so it can fit in our bedrooms."

"This is gonna be a law whether the President vetoes it or not. They have the votes in the Senate to override it."

"The Senate's not in session. The President could stick this in his pants pocket and it's vetoed."

"And it will come back in January and you will have to live through this twice. And you will lose both times. Ask me the question."

"He compared homosexuality to kleptomania and sex addition, Matt! The Majority Leader. The leader of your own party!"

---

[68] In "The Portland Trip", S2E7.

"Ask me the question, Josh."

"How can you be a member of this party???"

"You've been holding that in for way too long, man."

"This party who says that who you are is against the law!"

Congressman Skinner is an exemplar of that all-too-rare phenomenon, a gay Republican politician. Rare enough when the show was on the air; even more so today.

And this, an exchange in the Roosevelt Room between Sam and several military officers, discussing the possibility of lifting the ban on gays serving in the armed forces:[69]

"We know the report," one of the officers is replying to Sam. "A lot of the cases you're talking about is the gays being discharged, came from voluntary statements-"

"And a lot of these are not voluntary statements, not by any definition given by any civilian court in this country. It is not a voluntary statement when it's given to a psychotherapist, as in the case of former Marine corporal David Blessing. It is not a voluntary statement when it's made into a personal diary, as in the case of former West Point cadet Nicole Garrison. It is not when it's made after being asked, as in the case of master chief officer Diane Kelli. And it is not when it is coerced out of a service member through fear... through intimidation, through death threats, in terms of criminal prosecution, as in the case of former Air Force Major Bob Kiddis, former Marine gunnery sergeant Kevin Keys, and four sailors aboard the *USS Essex*."

"Sam, you take care of your guys; we'll take care of ours."

"You're not taking care of your guys. Your guys are out looking for jobs."

"Those weren't our guys."

And with that, Admiral Fitzwallace, Chairman of the Joint Chiefs, enters the room.

"We're discussing gays in the military, huh? What do you think?"

"Sir, we're here to help the White House form a possible-"

"I know. I'm asking you what you think."

---

[69] In "Let Bartlet Be Bartlet", S1E19.

"Sir, we're not prejudiced toward homosexuals."

"You just don't want to see them serving in the Armed Forces?"

"No sir, I don't."

"'Cause they pose a threat to unit discipline and cohesion."

"Yes sir."

"That's what I think, too. I also think the military wasn't designed to be an instrument of social change."

"Yes sir."

"The problem with that is that's what they were saying about me, 50 years ago. Blacks shouldn't serve with whites. It would disrupt the unit. You know what? It *did* disrupt the unit. The unit got over it. The unit changed. I'm an admiral in the US Navy and Chairman of the Joint Chiefs of Staff. Beat that with a stick!"

This is one issue area where we can gleefully acknowledge social progress beyond *The West Wing*'s expectations. During the show's run, legally-recognized same-sex marriage began in Massachusetts (2004) and made its way to the other 49 states over the next decade. These rulings got a boost from the Equal Protection Clause of the Fourteenth Amendment, which says no state can make a law that abridges the privileges and immunities of anyone in any other state.

In 1972, the Supreme Court didn't yet have any appetite for the issue, though civil rights groups had already begun clamoring for it. Two decades later, the Hawaii Supreme Court ruled that is was unconstitutional for the state to abridge marriage on the basis of sex, which led to the backlash of the federal Defense of Marriage Act of 1996 (referenced in *The West Wing*). And in 2003, Massachusetts repeated Hawaii's declaration, clearing the way for more state-based access to same-sex marriage: public opinion turned, leading to its legalization in 36 of the 50 states.

As of 2021, citizens in 47 of the 50 states supported same-sex marriage. Only Mississippi and Arkansas had majority opposition (Alabama was split). Sixty percent of Americans polled said they would be okay with their child marrying someone of their own gender.

As for gays in the military, the "Don't Ask, Don't Tell" policy implemented under President Bill Clinton in 1993 was repealed on

September 10, 2011. Conservative Republicans running for the White House in 2012 – Michele Bachmann, Rick Santorum, and Rick Perry – all called for its restoration. Newt Gingrich called for its repeal to be reviewed.

And in September 2021, President Joe Biden announced that benefits would be made available for service members discharged for being gay prior to "Don't Ask, Don't Tell".

All of this followed from a profound shift in public opinion. In 1993, only 44% of Americans polled supported gays in the military; in 2010, that number had climbed to 77%.

If only every issue taken up by *The West Wing* could show that much progress!

"The streets of heaven are too crowded with angels, but every time we think we have measured our capacity to meet a challenge, we look up and we're reminded that that capacity may well be limitless. this is a time for American heroes. We will do what is hard. We will achieve what is great. This is a time for American heroes and we reach for the stars."

~President Bartlet

"With that, I'm going to get a cupcake."

Women's Rights

Aaron Sorkin has been criticized, more than once, for not writing female characters as insightfully as his male ones, despite the admiration heaped upon CJ and Abbey Bartlet and others from *The Newsroom, Sports Night*, etc. And when it comes to *The West Wing*, there is some ambiguity in how women in general fit into the framework of the greater good.

It's not that there's any ambiguity about women's right or gender roles in the show's rhetoric or Sorkin's dialog; *The West Wing* is very clearly pro-women, as liberal as can be, and often disdainful of patriarchal attitudes. It's that we don't see the focus on the issue that we so often see in *The West Wing*'s surveys of other issues. Women's rights, in Sorkin's hands, often spiral off to the periphery.

That said, the occasions when the show gets into that territory are spirited and interesting. And no one is more spirited or interesting on this subject that Ainsley Hayes.

"'Equality of rights under the law shall not be denied or abridged by the United States or any state on account of sex,'" Sam quotes from the Equal Rights Amendment, having learned to his horror that Ainsley is not in favor of it. "*...shall not be abridged or denied on account of sex. Very* dangerous language! This must be stopped! What could possibly be your problem with the ERA?"[70]

"It's redundant."

"It's redundant?"

"Look, I'm a low maintenance lady," she casually replies. "I've got the 14th Amendment. I'm fine! The 14th Amendment which says a citizen of the United States is anyone that's born here – that's

---

[70] In "17 People", S2E18.

me - and that no citizen can be denied due process. I'm covered. Make a law for somebody else."

"If the Amendment's redundant, what's your problem if it's passed or not?"

"Because I'm a Republican! Have we met? I believe that every time the federal government hands down a new law, it leaves for the rest of us a little less freedom. So I say, let's just stick to the ones we absolutely need to have water come out of the faucet and our cars not stolen. That is my problem with passing a redundant law."

"How can you have an objection to something that says-"

"Because it's humiliating! A new amendment that we vote on, declaring that I am equal under the law to a man. I am mortified to discover there's reason to believe I wasn't before. I am a citizen of this country. I am not a special subset in need of your protection. I do not have to have to have my rights handed down to me by a bunch of old, white men. The same Article 14 that protects you protects me; and I went to law school - just to make sure."

It's an interesting argument, and serves up some great back-and-forth between her and Sam, who have moved from their initial rocky start on Capital Beat to an almost playful sibling relationship. And she gets more interesting still in "Night Five",[71] when Sam has made the wolfish comment "You're enough to make a good dog break his leash," the inanity of which tickles Ainsley, gets an eye roll from Charlie, but offends bullpen staffer Celia:

"He's not a sexist," Ainsley tells Celia in Sam's defense.

"I'm surprised you're willing to let him sexuality diminish your power," Celia replies, with a touch of condescension.

"I don't even know what that means," Ainsley fires back. "And I think you think I'm made out of candy glass, Celia. If somebody says something that offends you, tell them, but all women don't have to think alike. I like it when the guys tease me. It's an inadvertent show of respect that I'm on the team and I don't mind it when it gets sexual. And you know why? I like sex! I don't think that whatever sexuality I may have diminishes my power. I think it enhances it."

"And what kind of feminism do you call that?"

---

[71] S3E13.

"My kind."

"It's called Lipstick Feminism," Ginger helpfully interjects. "I call it Stiletto Feminism."

"Isn't the point that Sam wouldn't have been able to find another way to be chummy with a woman who wasn't sexually appealing?"

"He would be able to, but that isn't the point. The point is that sexual revolution tends to get in the way of actual revolution. Nonsense issues distract attention away from real ones: pay equity, child care, honest-to-god sexual harassment and in this case, a speech in front of the UN General Assembly. So, you -" She looks at Sam - "twenty-five percent on the assessments for Category A. You-" She looks at Charlie - "I don't know what your thing is." She turns to Celia. "And you, stop trying to take the fun out of my day! With that, I'm going to get a cupcake."

CJ is, of course, the Bartlet Administration's standard-bearer on women's issues, made subtly clear in the following exchange with Bruno Gianelli aboard Air Force One:[72]

"Yesterday, the First Lady appeared on KCAL, which is a local LA station. She was asked about the suspension of her medical license and she said something like, 'I'm just a wife and mother.'"

"And that has been interpreted in some circles as *merely* a wife and mother?"

"This is Flint Aldridge, a Southern Baptist radio host: 'This is another sign that Abbey Bartlet is a liberal elitist feminist.'"

"*Elitist feminist* - you can't do that to the English language."

"And this is from Janet Ritchie," CJ continues, referring to the wife of Bartlet's Republican opponent in the re-elect, Florida Governor Rob Ritchie.

"Janet Ritchie went on the record?"

"'Being a wife and a mother are the most rewarding roles I've ever played. I think Abbey Bartlet and I have two different ambitions.'"

"Ooh, she won fifty dollars. Said the secret word right there - ambition. Phyllis Schlafly and Ann Coulter are going to have a square dance."

---

[72] In "20 Hours in America, Pt. I", S4E1.

"Anyway, it's waiting for us down on the ground."

"I love it when the women get involved."

But Amy Gardner captures the show's best take on women's rights in "Debate Camp",[73] when Josh turns to her for a statement on the subject in a cell phone call.

"I don't know what you want me to say," she tells him after thinking about it. "I want women to have help from the government. I want women to earn what men earn. I want everyone to earn enough so that everyone can make the right choice for their family, and after that, it's none of your business who stays home and who goes to work. You don't know more about raising a family than I do."

Amy gives this response to Josh because she can't come up with the answer he wants. But, of course, it's *exactly* the answer he wants. And it expresses, in a short four sentences, exactly how most Americans feel about women's rights and their expectations of their government.

In the real world, coinciding with the years just before the Bartlet presidency in *The West Wing*, women's rights took several leaps forward.

The first of these was subtle but significant. In 1994, the Gender Equity in Education Act was adopted by Congress, pursuant to training teachers in gender equity and promoting stronger math and science education for girls. It also provided counseling for pregnant teenagers and included preventative measures against sexual harassment.

More publicly that same year, the Violence Against Women Act funded services for women who were victims of rape or domestic violence, also offering civil rights remediation for gender-related crimes. It provided sensitivity training for police and court officials, and established a national 24-hour hotline for battered women.

In 1997, Madeleine Albright became the first female Secretary of State.

---

[73] S4E5.

In 2005, Condoleezza Rice because the first black female Secretary of State.

In 2007, Nancy Pelosi became the first female Speaker of the House.

In 2009, Sonio Sotomayor became the first Hispanic female justice of the Supreme Court.

In 2016, Hillary Clinton because the first female nominee for president of the United States.

In 2013, the ban against women in military combat roles was finally lifted.

When the Violence Against Women Act was reauthorized in 2013, it was extended to cover women on Native American tribal lands.

In 2017, the Women's March – a four-million person movement occurring in locations all around the US, the largest single-day protest in US history – was held on the day after Trump's inauguration, under the banner, "Women's rights are human rights."

In 2021, Kamala Harris was sworn in as the first female (and first black) vice-president of the United States.

In 2022, President Joe Biden signed the reauthorization of the VAWA.

On the other hand...

Also in 2022, the Roberts Court brought Amy Gardner's worst nightmare to life, reversing *Roe v. Wade* after almost 50 years, with the Dobbs decision. But that one's so big and important, we'll be spending an entire chapter on it later.

In the meantime, here's the work still to be done. According to the National Women's History Project,

- The gender gap in pay is still where it was when Ainsley was arguing the ERA with Sam (20%);
- One-third of all single mothers in the US live in poverty;
- One-third of all women in the US experience abuse;
- 4.7 million women experience violence by their partner;
- Women in the US military are more likely to be raped by their male peers than they are to be killed in combat;

- In US government, women only comprise 28% of Congress, and hold only 12 state governor's offices;
- In the Fortune 500, less than 10% of CEOs are women.

Even so, we can be sure that CJ and Amy would call it progress. And they'd be all over the Dobbs decision.

"Education is the silver bullet!"

Public Education Policy

Leo has been screwing with Sam. His daughter Mallory likes Sam and asks him out, so Leo sets Sam up to look bad by leaking a memo Sam wrote as opposition prep, putting him on the wrong side of public education – toxic, as Mallory is a school teacher.[74]

When Sam finally reveals his true feelings about publication, it comes out like this:

"Mallory, education is the silver bullet. Education is *everything!* We don't need little changes, we need gigantic, monumental changes! Schools should be palaces. The competition for the best teachers should be fierce. They should be making six-figure salaries. School should be incredibly expensive for government and absolutely free of charge to its citizens, just like national defense! *That's* my position. I just haven't figured out how to do it yet."

Sam isn't alone, of course; President Bartlet put forth a $1.5 package of education reform legislation in his first term after vetoing an anemic one proposed by the Republican Congress;[75] President Bartlet once called himself "the Education President";[76] Congressman Matt Santos, running to succeed President Bartlet, made public education reform the centerpiece of his policy portfolio.

In hindsight, neither Mallory nor Sam realized how good they had it. Since the turn of the century, public education – and public schoolteachers, in particular – have been under increasing attack from right-wing politicians and media. It's no longer a question of

---

[74] In "Six Meetings Before Lunch", S1E18.

[75] In "In This White House", S2E4.

[76] In "Manchester, Pt. II", S3E2.

finding ways to improve public education; it's now a question of saving it altogether.

The Right's war on public education

There are two prominent prongs in the skewer with which the Right has prodded public education in recent years: the push to privatize it, and the quest to censor it.

The privatization prong has been largely constructed out of *voucher schemes* – government-funded certificates made available to families that allow them to go to private schools (including religious schools).[77]

The math of voucher systems is simple: hundreds of millions of dollars are drained from public school students to pay the private school bills of a select few. Most public school educators are rigidly opposed to vouchers and determined to stop them.

This push was most prominent during the Trump Administration through his Secretary of Education Betsy DeVos, who was a stalwart champion of vouchers, and the administrations FY2018-19 budget etched it in stone. It called for $1.4 billion in funding for expansion of private school voucher programs, in a program that called for an eventual commitment of $20 billion annually.

(As a side note, this privatization push by conservatives is as much about ideology as it is social elitism; vouchers can fund school science programs that promote creationism, at US taxpayer expense.)

After leaving office, Trump called for the US Department of Education to be abolished altogether – a statement echoing one made by Betsy DeVos at the Moms for Liberty conference after leaving her cabinet post.

---

[77] *The West Wing* tackled this one in "Full Disclosure" (S5E15), when a school vouchers rider was attached to a bill and President Bartlet brought in the mayor of Washington, DC to discuss the ramifications – finding, to his surprise, that not only was the mayor becoming open-minded to voucher programs, but that his own body man Charlie had wished for the opportunities to attend a better school that vouchers would have enabled. In *The American President*, President Andrew Shepherd was staunchly opposed to them.

President Joe Biden's administration has fought to counter the damage done to public education by GOP presidents and politicians over the past two decades, putting forth his plan in April 2023 to invest $11 billion in education and ancillary services – which House Republicans promptly proposed to cut by almost 25%, gutting funding for low-income students (26 million of them), gutting support for students with disabilities (7.5 million), gutting mental health support for students (in an era when the Pew Research Center reported in 2018 that 57% of students are worried about being shot at school),[78] and eliminating or nearly eliminating Pell Grants for college undergraduates. The Republican proposal also sought to cancel President Biden's student debt relief.

The Republican war on teachers

Teachers themselves are increasingly the subject of perpetual attack at both the national and local levels. Already overworked, underpaid, and under-supported, they have been made out by politicians, right-wing media and conservative parent groups to be nefarious indoctrinators, poisoning the minds of children, unworthy of the respect they traditionally received. Denise Pope of Stanford University summed it up, saying that public schools have become "a pressure cooker for students and staff; and student and teacher stress feed of each other."

A study by the University of Missouri in 2018 put a number to it: "Ninety-three percent of elementary school teachers report they are 'highly stressed.'"

Since the advent of the Covid-19 pandemic, the loss of public schoolteachers has been 567,000, according to the Bureau of Labor Statistics. The new hire rate is at an all-time low, with 0.57 hires for each open position. The National Education Association released a poll in 2022 reporting that 55% of teachers polled plan to leave the field earlier than they had originally expected to, 80% of them

---

[78] Since the Colorado Columbine High School shooting of 1999, more than 187,000 students have been exposed to gun violence at school.

feeling that the evacuation of the profession has increased the workload of all those who remain.

The Economic Policy Institute reported in 2022 that almost every state has experienced substantial losses of public schoolteachers, with 16 states losing 5% or more.

An award-winning Michigan teacher of 17 years who is also planning to leave summed it up:

"The essential problem for myself and most teachers right now is this: If we choose the profession that we love, that we believe in, that serves our communities and the future of our country, we are also often choosing exhaustion, debt, poor health, ridicule, and no time or energy for our own families."

In Wisconsin, this diaspora began years ago when then-Governor Scott Walker stripped public sector workers of their collective bargaining rights, resulting in staffing shortages everywhere. This left the Milwaukee Teachers' Education Association begging long-term teachers not to leave.

We are reminded of how differently President Bartlet's team approached the problem, in "The Portland Trip", conceiving a plan to draw new public schoolteachers into the profession by paying for their educations, as the military does for doctors and lawyers, in exchange for three years' public school service.

Ron DeSantis and anti-woke

For all the open meddling in public schools done by conservatives and Republicans over the decades, the attacks on higher education had been largely limited to defunding efforts; the schools themselves remained free to teach without government interference, as they were meant to be.

But now this, too, is fair game for the right. The pacesetter here has been Florida Gov. Ron DeSantis, who launched relentless attacks on higher education in his state as a way of attracting the Trump base to his campaign for the 2024 presidential election.

These attacks took the familiar form of demonizing that which he sought to take over – decrying the state's colleges and universities as havens of liberal extremism and "woke" indoctrination in dire need of overhaul. DeSantis proceeded to abolish DEI (diversity/equality/inclusion), folding racism into an authoritarian power play. (Those DEI programs had been mandated, ironically, by a Republican-appointed board of governors.)

His attacks included a proposal to curtail the faculty tenure system, a cornerstone of both free speech and scholastic independence, as well as state-imposed curricula including "actual history and actual philosophy that have shaped western civilization" - the conservative versions, in other words, free of "critical race theory" (which doesn't exist in college curricula), gender studies, intersectionality, and other topics that ran counter to his cultural worldview.

His testbed was New College of Florida, a public liberal arts college in Sarasota. The changes he proposed drew harsh condemnation from both educators in the state and observers around the nation.

"The call to overhaul New College is part of an orchestrated set of moves to undercut the principles of public education, of freedom of speech across the US," Amy Reid, a professor of French and director of the college's gender studies program, told *The Guardian*. "What's happening in New College is not just another anecdote from Florida. The suggestion that we adopt a curriculum based on Hillsdale's Eurocentric and explicitly religious, so-called classical model challenges not only the principle of free speech, but also the goal of fostering an engaged and informed citizenry."

The Guardian also wrote that "Prominent members of the country's higher education sector see in DeSantis's so-called blueprint for academic reform a thinly-veiled and continuing bid to lure voters away from Trump's base as the governor contemplates a direct challenge to the former president's already launched candidature."

"This is about building a national political brand by engaging in the culture wars, and as far as he is concerned, the more outrage and media coverage, the better," said Brian Rosenberg, a visiting professor at the Harvard Graduate School of Education and president emeritus of Minnesota's Macalester College. "The colleges and students in Florida are simply collateral damage, about which he is unconcerned."

V. Jo Hsu wrote in March 2023[79] that the DeSantis bill "offers a terrifying preview of conservatives' agenda for higher education. The bill, which was introduced in February, would grant Florida's Board of Governors sweeping control over the state's public universities and transform the state's public education system into an incubator for far-right politics.

"These measures will compromise students' education, prevent schools from attracting and retaining faculty and funding and increase bias in higher education. In Florida, professors have already begun censoring important course content, searching for other jobs and discouraging other faculty from coming to their state.

"This weaponization of education is a core component of conservatives' political strategy. That's not an opinion; it's a quote. At the New College of Florida, the state's Republican Governor Ron DeSantis filled the board of trustees—which governs the school— with conservative activists who ousted the college president. They replaced him with Richard Corcoran, a Republican politician who once told a conservative audience, 'Education is our sword, that's our weapon.'

"Conservatives' aggressive takeover of higher education requires dismantling DEI and so-called CRT programs because access to diverse materials and social contexts fosters critical thinking. Overwhelming evidence shows that research teams with varying backgrounds, areas of expertise, thinking styles and skill sets are not only more innovative, but come up with more accurate predictions and better solutions.

"Dismantling DEI programs will hinder far more than classroom content. DEI represents a wide range of initiatives that ensure people can participate more fully in their roles as students, faculty and staff. DEI is central to resources like food pantries; support for veterans, first-generation, rural and disabled students; mental and physical health care; and offices that address harassment or violence.

"The United States is moving toward a more diverse future, regardless of conservatives' regressive campaigns. A majority of K-12 students are now people of color. The number of people

---

[79] In *The Progressive.*

identifying as LGBTQ+ increases with each generation. And 26 percent of US adults identify as having a disability.

"We need university resources and governance that will help grow these spaces alongside new generations of thinkers and leaders. Without a staunch defense of diversity, equity and inclusion, conservatives will not only 'conquer' but destroy public higher education."

Beyond Florida

The DeSantis assault on higher education in Florida reflects the disdain for public higher education held by Republicans generally. Among those who want to see funding for public colleges further reduced, 20% want to see it eliminated altogether (the percentage among Trump supporters is higher). Their justification is a belief, cultivated by right-wing media, that higher educational institutions are hotbeds of liberal indoctrination and propaganda, and that education should not be publicly funded in any case.

A 2022 Pew Research survey reported that 76% of Democrats consider college and university education to be a plus for the country; conversely, the same percentage of Republicans think colleges and universities affect the country negatively.

Irene Mulvey, president of the American Association of University Professors, reported that more than 50 bills attacking DEI programs have been introduced across 23 states.

"A lot of it is made up," she said. "There are real problems in higher education to fix, like decades of underfunding. There is the problem of contingent faculty that have no academic freedom. So to argue that this is indoctrination in higher education is completely made up. There's no evidence that's happening. The rationales for these bills are a completely made-up mischaracterization of what's happening in order to drag higher education into the culture wars, to make higher education a political talking point for voters who may not be paying attention to what's really going on.

"They want higher education to become a football like [critical race theory] or abortion. They're dragging higher education into the culture wars to serve a political agenda. The damage it will do to higher education is the real story. They may be doing this just to get some votes, but the damage to public higher education will take decades to undo. The damage to higher education is essentially a domino and democracy itself is at the end of this line of dominoes."

The draft of the FY2024 Labor, Health and Human Services, Education, and Related Agencies funding bill released in July 2023 by the Republicans on the House Appropriations Committee took a meat cleaver to funding for education and job training, also decimating research monies. It cuts 2024 total funding by 28% of 2023 levels, making it the lowest appropriation for those agencies since 2008.

It slashes K-12 support, abandons low-income workers seeking higher education or job training, cuts funding for cancer research, mental health research and neurological research, slashes support for ongoing public health crises in HIV/AIDS, opioid addiction and mental health, and cuts women's health programs, maternal and child health in particular, with partisan riders attaching reproductive health.

"When 161 House Republicans voted earlier this year to eliminate all K-12 funding at the Department of Education, I was horrified, but that was just the beginning. Now, in the midst of a teacher shortage, they have introduced a bill that would kick 220,000 teachers from classrooms. We are witnessing a widespread attack on public education that should horrify all of us," said Appropriations Committee Ranking Member Rosa DeLauro. "Regardless of age or stage in life, this bill means you cannot count on government for any help. It limits women's access to abortion while stripping maternal health services and making diapers more expensive. It decimates access to preschool, education, and job training. People can only hope they do not get cancer or need mental health services - you will not find support from House Republicans. These awful cuts will make it very hard for people and should not even be considered by this committee."

Overall, it's a pretty bleak picture. Public education is under attack like never before, and the warfare is open and obvious. It makes *The West Wing*'s contacts with the topic seem almost quaint.

And yet, education *is* the silver bullet; it absolutely *is* a crucial part of the only remedy for the toxic thinking that is growing all around us. Ignorance is a bulwark against knowledge, and knowledge is essential to positive change. Reducing ignorance, then, is essential to our forward motion as a nation.

We can't change the minds of the willfully ignorant; but we can resolve to do everything in our power to make certain our children grow up knowledgeable, well-informed, and possessing a worldview that includes a healthy and positive future on its horizon.

"What did liberals do that was so offensive to the Republican party? I'll tell you what they did. Liberals ended segregation. Liberals passed the Civil Rights Act, the Voting Rights Act. Liberals created Medicare. Liberals passed the Clean Air Act, the Clean Water Act. What did Conservatives do? They opposed them on every one of those things. Every one. So when you try to hurl that label at my feet, 'Liberal,' as if it were something to be ashamed of, something dirty, something to run away from, it won't work, Senator, because I will pick up that label and I will wear it as a badge of honor."

~Matt Santos

LemonLyman.com

White House Social Media Disasters

The perils of social media are known to us all at this point, regardless of our station or role in the world, thanks to almost a decade and a half of Facebook, Twitter and their siblings. We have all found ourselves misunderstood and misunderstanding; most of us have gotten jacked up over some post or tweet or meme that pushed our buttons; and more than a few of us have said something we shouldn't.

This kind of trouble is impossible to avoid today, but in 2002, when the third-season episode "The US Poet Laureate"[80] aired, Facebook and Twitter weren't yet a thing (the Internet itself had only been open to commercial traffic for a decade). Their precursors – forum websites and bulletin boards – were the digital places where people gathered to e-chat, commiserate, vent, and snark off. It's fair to say that not everyone watching the episode the first time it aired even knew what a forum site was. Josh himself seemed to be encountering the phenomenon for the first time, given his lack of clarity about its potential for calamity...

Josh passes Donna's desk and finds her surrounded by Margaret, Ginger and other assistants. They have stumbled across a forum website, and can't get enough of it.

"It's your fan site," Donna explains.

"What are you talking about?"

"There's a website devoted to all things Josh."

"You're kidding me."

"No." He leans in.

"'LemonLyman.com'?"

---

[80] S3E16.

"You have fans, Josh. Not many of them, from the looks of it, but what they lack in numbers, they more than make up for in fervor."

LemonLyman.com, it seems, hosts discussions of Josh's media appearances, lists sightings of him around Washington, and features a special section where the enamored discuss their Josh Fantasy Date.

Josh scatters the assistants, but later asks Donna to sit and help him post on the site, which he clearly has been perusing.

"It's a bad idea," Donna cautions him.

"Why?"

"You don't know these people."

"Neither do you."

"Oh, yes, I do!"

"What's wrong with them?"

"Nobody knows."

Thinking that the LemonLyman.com dwellers are praiseworthy for taking an interest in government, Josh insists on getting involved, instructing Donna to type a post correcting what he believes is a misunderstanding of something he had said on Nightline. Despite Donna's "Please don't do this...people on these sites tend to be a little hysterical," his response is posted.

"What Josh doesn't know is that some of these people haven't taken their medication," she says to the fourth wall. "Let's see what happens now!"

Social media is here to stay

When Josh discovered social media, in a year before it was even called that, the phenomenon was peripheral at best - today, of course, it is not only ubiquitous but immersive; many if not most of us participate daily, and almost no one doesn't participate at all – but the rise of social media as part of everyday life, let alone its deployment as a political tool, would be the better part of a decade in coming.

Political websites and campaign emails have been around for more than two decades. As soon as these tools became available, it was inevitable that politicians entrenched and aspiring would leverage them as communication channels, connections to the electorate. And so they have been, as long as they've been around. Per Diana Owen, in *Towards a New Enlightenment? A Transcendent Decade,*

"The public gained greater political agency through technological affordances that allowed them to react to political events and issues, communicate directly to candidates and political leaders, contribute original news, images, videos, and political content, and engage in political activities, such as working on behalf of candidates, raising funds, and organizing protests. At the same time, journalists acquired pioneering mechanisms for reporting stories and reaching audiences. Politicians amassed new ways of conveying messages to the public, other elites, and the press, influencing constituents' opinions, recruiting volunteers and donors, and mobilizing voters."

But the true date of birth of social media as a real political tool occurred during the 2008 Obama campaign, well after Josh Lyman's rude awakening. That campaign took the novel approach of using hi-tech methodology and tools to muster what was essentially a grass-roots campaign. Via Facebook, Twitter and other platforms, the Obama team was able to radically ratchet up both the volume and speed of messaging to the electorate. When all was said and done, they had out-messaged Republican opponent John McCain 3-to-1.

Beyond messaging, there's the analytics: by bringing voters into frequent online engagement, it became possible to know 1) how often each one was showing up, 2) what content was engaging them, and 3) where they'd landed from and where they'd gone next. This information was invaluable in fine-tuning messaging for micro-segmented voter audiences. Needless to say, this was Political Moneyball; once these techniques had entered the water supply, no campaign dared eschew them.

With one obvious exception.

The dictatorial ruler's thumb

Josh is in his office, browsing LemonLyman.com (as we might guess, he just can't help himself).

"Donna? Something weird is happening here."

Donna sticks her head in his office.

"They don't seem to be taking my response in the spirit in which it was intended."

This is no surprise to Donna. Josh is learning for the first time how most Internet forums work.

"Seems to be a very unusual social structure," he has noticed. "There's a leader who seems to pride herself on her organizational skills and a certain amount of discipline."

"Right," Donna nods. "That's what's called a 'control freak'."

"She seems to do an awful lot of scolding," Josh continues. "'You've posted in the wrong place'... 'Stay on topic, people'... 'Don't use capital letters'... but that's not the problem."

He reads directly from a post the moderator wrote:

"'Someone needs to deal with Josh's planet-sized ego, by teaching him Government 101. Who made him overlord of the Democratic Party?'; and someone else writes, 'Is Josh delusional, or is he actively trying to destroy the separation of powers?'"

"Well, are you?"

"No!"

"Then turn off the computer, shut these people up, and let's get back to work."

"I think I need to clarify my original post..."

...and the whole thing escalates. Josh's response is snarky, condescending, and far less polite than his original comment. He goes so far as to defy the moderator.

"See, I think these are good people, by and large," he says to Donna after she types his post, "but they've come under the thumb of a dictatorial ruler. So, as with a small Central American country, my role is to incite the people to topple her..."

Josh has tripped and fallen into the social media minefield that has maimed so many of us over the years.

When Donald Trump entered the arena in 2015, he already had many years of Twitter experience under his thumbs. He had been tweeting to a hungry audience day in and day out on all manner of topics, from Anthony Weiner's sex life to President Obama's birth certificate, with a consistency perhaps unmatched by any other activity in which he ever indulged.

He knew, first-hand, that people now spend more time on social media than they do watching television or reading the paper or listening to the radio; he knew, because (with the sole exception of Fox News), he is himself such a person. Social media is the place to be if you want to be seen – which he always does, more than anything; and when he got serious about running for president (to the degree that it has ever been truly serious to him), he knew that social media is where the voters are.

But there was no strategy, no plan, no systematic deployment of targeted messaging; no microsegmentation of his base, no analytics, no fine-tuning. There was only Trump and tweet and whatever happens next.

Trump's effectiveness in ascending to office and using social media to connect directly with his base, bypassing the usual channels, filters, and checks/balances, must be honestly rated as effective – every bit as effective as the Obama campaign use of social media (though to radically different ends). In the latter case, the point of social media was to improve communication between the campaign and the electorate – to message more effectively and to hear what the electorate was thinking and feeling with greater sensitivity. On the Trump channel, the only real communication is whatever Trump is feeling in the moment, and his reactions (when feuding) to whoever is pushing back at him. There are no two-way streets in Trumpville.

What does all of this say about the real political landscape? There are two takeaways that we can map to Josh Lyman.

1. *Authority, in a social media context, is a murky proposition at best.* Perhaps the single biggest social feature of social media is lack of consequence: one can participate at whatever level one wishes – lurking, commenting occasionally, participating regularly and actively, indulging in snark and antagonism, intentionally triggering fear and anger in others, going full-on troll – and suffer nothing more than a time-out if caught. Why is this so? Because no one has any real power; even site moderators and administrators,

like LemonLyman.com's "dictatorial ruler," can do nothing more than scold or, at worst, block Josh; she can have no meaningful impact on him in the real world. What must be noted, however, is that the reverse is also true; Josh tries to parade his power and knowledge for the group, as though it represents actual power in the ethereal realm of a website - and he gets nowhere. No one in social media – *not even a president!!!* - has any real power in that domain.

2. *Social media is too shallow for effective confrontation.* Josh's attempt to throw his weight around on social media presages Donald Trump's annexation of it a decade later. Trump is Josh on steroids, with all sorts of horrific malignancy and unshackled dysphoria layered over the arrogance. Trump is the global pacesetter for online social dominance, trying to subdue his opponents and coddle his sycophants with his perpetual tweetstorm tirades and prevarications. But, again, even the planet's most prominent social dominator has no real power in social media; one need only tune in for five minutes to observe Trump taking it in the shins from all sides, every time he tweets, by critics and mockers and antagonists of every variety – none with any apparent station. The Internet remains the Great Equalizer, in this regard, and Trump's failure to understand this is myopia of the most telling sort: nothing he says or does has any impact beyond the moment. He does his followers no good and his critics no harm with his outbursts; the medium itself is impotent, and so, by extension, is he: it's a schoolyard with no mudballs, a junior-high cafeteria with no mashed potatoes.

Put simply, confrontation in social media is pointless as a general rule – and certainly pointless for any elected leader. It's not built for that. Social dominance is the baring of teeth, the flashing of claw; social media possesses neither.

A Chief Bromden in every White House

Even in 2002, social media's leakage to other media had begun. A Josh feud on an Internet website would inevitably find its way to other channels.

"Oh, Josh?" CJ calls out in a West Wing corridor. He stops.

"The Federal Page of the *Washington Post* just called Carol to confirm that you're the Josh Lyman who stated on an Internet website that the White House could order a GAO review on anything it wants."

"...without threatening Separation of Powers, is what I was saying."

"You *posted on a website?*"

"I was communicating with the people."

Ah, *communicating with the people*. This is the justification that wafted through social media during the Trump administration, as the 45th posted with nauseating frequency, bypassing all official channels, filters, fact-checks and protocols – all to *communicate with the people*.

This is problematic for a number of reasons. First, Trump's use of social media isn't a supplement to other channels of *communication with the people*, as it was with President Obama – it is his *only* channel of communication. Oh, he sent a lieutenant to the White House Press Room on occasion to prevaricate on his behalf, but that occurred less in his administration than any previous one *by an order of magnitude*. Second, *communicate* is a dicey word in this context; Trump does not inform the people, he deliberately *mis*informs them. At this writing, he has lied to the public more than 20,000 times – and most of those lies traveled via Twitter. Finally, the Twitter user base isn't *the people*; it's his fan club, not even close to a representation of the electorate. Previous presidents have spoken to that electorate by television (on all three-plus networks, not just one), knowing they were getting the voters who loved them, hated them, and the ones who couldn't make up their minds; Trump tweets *precisely because* those who bother to follow him on Twitter are the only ones listening, with rare exception.

But back to Josh.

He tries to explain to CJ that the website is Crazytown, which of course doesn't surprise CJ at all.

"Let me explain something to you," she tells him. "This is sort of my field. The people on these sites? They're the cast of *One Flew Over the Cuckoo's Nest*. The muumuu-wearing Parliament smoker? That's Nurse Ratched. When Nurse Ratched is unhappy, the patients are unhappy. You? You're McMurphy. You swoop in there with your card games and your fishing trips-"

"I didn't swoop in! I came in exactly the same way everybody else did."

"Well, now I'm telling you to open the wardroom window and climb out before they give you a pre-frontal lobotomy, and I have to smother you with a pillow!"

"You're Chief Brom-"

"I'm Chief Bromden, yes, at this particular moment! I'm assigning an intern from the press office to that website. They're going to check it every night before they go home. If they discover you've been there, I'm going to shove a motherboard so far up your ass-"

"...technically, I outrank you-"

"-so far up your ass!"

Social media is an excellent, even ideal channel for engaging the electorate, and an essential one: it is an invaluable source of information that a wise leader requires in these uncertain, immediate days. Used intelligently, it can be that and more – a path to insight, a source of important information about the candidate for the voter, an avenue to inspiration and (in our dreams) a place of calm. *If* it's used intelligently.

If it isn't - well, there's one lesson Trump's Twitter account makes all too clear, it's that every White House needs a CJ. There should be someone in every administration empowered to monitor the president's social media activity, at all times.

It should even be a Cabinet position...

"We came out of the cave, and we looked over the hill, and we saw fire. And we crossed the ocean, and we pioneered the West, and we took to the sky. The history of man is hung on the timeline of exploration, and this is what's next!"

~Sam

"We're gonna listen to the experts."

White House Respect for Science and Reality

The White House staff's respect for CJ is, of course, well-earned. Press Secretary is one of the toughest jobs in all of politics, and those who hold the post must constantly walk a tightrope with no net – and there's a pool of piranha on one side and a velociraptor pen on the other.

The White House Press Room is where the world gets its clearest indication of what a president is thinking and who the president is listening to, based on what the press secretary passes along. And one specific domain of thought and deference has risen above all others in recent years: a president's respect for scientific truth.

At this writing, the threat of the coronavirus pandemic looms large, not only over the United States but the planet itself. And the parade of misinformation, disinformation and outright bullshit that has issued forth from the Trump White House press room has been staggering.

In fairness, that press room has seen less activity than any other administration in modern history, and one doesn't need any of its many press secretaries to know what Trump is thinking – all one needs is a Twitter account. But the questions of who a president listens to and whether or not we know about it are all the more pressing for the Trump Administration's disinterest in the views of experts.

When is it okay to lie from the podium?

As it turns out, the Bartlet White House isn't sinless when it comes to misleading the press. It happened for the first time when the CIA was caught napping as a massive armed confrontation between Indian and Pakistani troops suddenly erupted, and Bartlet and Leo and Toby elected to keep CJ out of the loop initially –

sending her into the press room, for all practical purposes, to lie.[81] Toby tried to smooth it over...

"I was warned that coming to talk to you might be insulting to your professionalism," he says upon entering her office.

"Well, you wouldn't want to do that." She's clearly still very pissed.

"I wasn't ready for the press yet," he says, as if that makes anything better.

"Could've told me that before sending me in there," she replies.

"CJ-"

"I flatly denied it," she says, cutting him off. "I said I was in the Oval Office ten minutes ago and nothing's going on."

"They don't think you lied to them."

"I know that," she answers. "They think you lied to me, which is what happened. They don't know me. I'm from nowhere. I was just starting to get credible. I was just starting to get their respect. You know how long it's going to take me to get it back?"

"There's a concern-"

"'Don't ask CJ, she doesn't know anything!'"

"-there is a concern that you're too friendly with the press."

"Really."

"We know it's important that you have a friendly relationship with them-"

"It's important for all of us!"

"I don't disagree."

"Does this have to do with Danny Concannon?"

"People see you with Danny-"

"This is outrageous!"

"This is one time, and if we erred, it's on the side of trying to-"

"You sent me in there uninformed so that I'd lie to the press-"

"We sent you in there uninformed because we thought there was a chance you couldn't."

Is it ever okay to lie to the press?

---

[81] In "Lord John Marbury", S1E11.

In the scene above, the consensus of Bartlet and Leo and Toby was that they needed to stall on speaking on the record about the India-Pakistan confrontation until they knew more about what was happening and had time to plan their response. For CJ to get the question and tell the truth would have been politically disastrous, eroding confidence in the White House for purely circumstantial reasons. Such a lie is ethically gray, but understandable.

Lying to the press for political reasons is one thing; what about changing the story when it's science, rather than politics, that are at stake?

Science denial isn't just routine in the US at this point; it seems to be a plank in the GOP platform. And taking an anti-science stance from a White House podium isn't simply failing to be forthcoming; it erodes public confidence in professional expertise. That goes beyond the moment – it can do lasting damage.

Leo himself indulges in this editing of science, having his own showdown with CJ Will Bailey reveals to the two of them that Reuters has a story saying that the White House deleted two paragraphs from an EPA report on energy usage because the language was critical of the coal industry.[82]

Leo tells Will and CJ that it was he who cut the paragraphs. CJ wants to back-pedal it, but Leo stands firm: "'The report will reflect administration views.' That's the line."

CJ gets the question in the next press briefing.

"Sources at the EPA say the White House censored language from a report critical of coal-based energy. Does the White House feel that's appropriate?"

"The White House feels the EPA report will reflect administration views," CJ dutifully replies.

"Not the EPA's views. Their draft cited stunted trees, poisoned fish and wildlife as just some of the problems with coal. Hasn't this president always-"

"The final report will lay out views on a range of issues."

"Why did the White House tamper with an independent report?"

"I've addressed that."

---

[82] In "Constituency of One", S5E5.

"No, you haven't. Why is all independent analysis subject to White House censorship?"

"I don't accept your premise."

"Doesn't the EPA have the right-"

"I'm sure you all look forward to reading the actual report."

"I've read both drafts, the censored one and the original. Are you defending-"

"If there was interference with an independent report, that was obviously a mistake."

CJ, surfing for dear life toward a beach she doesn't want to be on, has now incurred Leo's wrath.

"They had both drafts," she explains to Leo later. "There was nothing I could do."

"I gave you the line. Who said you could drop it?"

They proceed to argue over "clean coal," which CJ considers mythical, but Leo defends on the basis of less environmentally harmful byproducts.

"When I give you the line, that's the line," he says definitively.

"Not when no one will believe it."

"You're going to put out a statement in your own name," he declares. "It's going to say what you should have said in that briefing room, that we stand behind that report."

"That's saying I wasn't speaking for this White House," she replies.

"You weren't," he says. "On my desk within the hour."

Ouch.

A War on Science

"Although scientific input to the government is rarely the only factor in public policy decisions, this input should always be weighed from an objective and impartial perspective to avoid perilous consequences. Indeed, this principle has long been adhered to by presidents and administrations of both parties in forming and implementing policies. The administration of George W. Bush has, however, disregarded this principle."

~"Restoring Scientific Integrity in Policymaking", the Union of Concerned Scientists

The Right in the US has been growing steadily more authoritarian since Goldwater – and science isn't the authoritarian's friend. Social dominance is about emotion, and facts are very inconvenient when emotions are at stake.

The GOP's pushback against science, learned testimony and professional expertise began with Reagan, when deregulation was the main course of the Right's legislative agenda and those pesky scientific experts kept introducing inconvenient facts into deregulation proceedings. But the GOP's anti-science penchant really hit its stride in 2001, with the Bush II administration.

While by no means the instigator of the Bush anti-science agenda, White House Science Advisor John Marburger was certainly its most visible exponent of it. It was he who responded to the Union of Concerned Scientists when they issued the document quoted above. That document, signed by more than 60 scientists and officials, highlighted the administration's systematic distortions of information, suppression of reports, and ideological selectivity in advisory panel appointments. It was a damning document, underscoring that the Bush White House represented a new low in the dismantling of professional expertise in policymaking.

Chris Mooney documents the clash between Marburger and his UCS critics in 2005's *The Republican War on Science*, a fact-packed, penetrating disclosure of the Right's steady erosion of public faith in the integrity of science for political ends. He lists luminaries Paul Ehrlich, E.O. Wilson and Republican environmentalist Russell Train among the UCS signatories, and details egregious, persistent malfeasance in the Bush White House's handling of scientific input into policy questions.

This malfeasance included modifications to the Endangered Species Act that made it harder to formally classify species and habitats in peril, over the objections of biologists; the jaw-dropping (and, in hindsight, outlandish) assertion that there was a connection between abortion and breast cancer; and documentation of the administration's cherry-picking of advisory panelists, based on their friendliness to conservative doctrine.

Marburger – a scientist himself, and a good one – became the public face of the Bush White House in responding to the UCS, whose missive had made its way to every major news outlet. His replies were not those of a scientist, however, but a spinner - laced with evasions, missed points, and furtive misdirection. The UCS, for its part, grew louder, and found allies in Congress willing to sound the alarm – including Congressman Henry Waxman, who characterized the Bush Administration's manipulations as "nothing more than the political creation of scientific uncertainty."

The most egregious of Marburger's sins, in the harsh light of history, was his politicization of climate science, which artfully blurred the uncertainty lines by illuminating actual uncertainties about climate change while completely failing to mention the strong consensual conclusions of the scientific community. In this, he was following his boss's lead, but it put the lie to his perpetual claim that he was just a messenger – certainly *not* a spinner! - and his denials that he had any trace of a partisan agenda.

"Such flagrant misrepresentation goes far beyond mere dishonesty," wrote Mooney. "It demonstrates a gross disregard for the welfare of the American public, who Bush represent[ed], and for the population of the entire globe, whose fate depends in large measure on the behavior of the American behemoth."

In late 2004, the *Washington Post* reported that the Bush White House had endeavored to suppress the Arctic Climate Impact Assessment, the scientific work of eight collaborating nations, with 300 participating scientists, and that it had "repeatedly resisted even mild language that would endorse the report's scientific findings."

The effects of the Bush White House assault on science remain to this day, of course; even a pro-science Democratic president like Barack Obama faced a confused, untrusting public, making the justification of sound policy all the more difficult.

Obama's Pandemics

Presidential dismissal or downplaying of scientific expertise over climate change (or any other public policy issue, for that matter) is certainly foolish, but it's not hard to see why much of the public lets it pass; though the long-term consequences are catastrophic (perhaps even existential), they are years, perhaps decades in the future. Even the near-term impact fails to register in the minds of many; climate change is, to a large degree, abstract. Put another way, it's hard for some people to be afraid of what they can't see in front of them.

Public health risks are another matter. Pandemics, for instance, are both immediate and all too visible, as the world is learning as of this writing; the consequences are all around us, in the deaths of those afflicted, the daily barrage of media attention, the all-pervasive reminders like masks and hand sanitizer. If we drop that immediacy and threat into the mix with the conditions already mentioned – political expediency and the often-uncomfortable inconvenience of scientific fact – we're in a whole new territory.

And pandemics are just the highest-profile of the many public health concerns that present these days. Whether the threat is large or small, the question remains: Is it permissible, or even conscionable, to deny science and the advice of medical experts when public health is at stake?

The West Wing tackled this one in "Ellie",[83] an episode focusing on President Bartlet's middle daughter, a medical student. After Dr. Millicent Griffith, the Surgeon General and a Bartlet family friend, says in an Internet interview that marijuana does not pose the same health risks as tobacco or alcohol, a firestorm erupts all around her, as this statement is at odds with the Bartlet Administration's negative stance on legalization. Matters become worse when Ellie Bartlet publicly comes to Griffith's defense: "My father won't fire the Surgeon General. He would never do that."

Now the president is fighting battles on two fronts: dealing with the political fallout from Dr. Griffith's apparent contradiction of

---

[83] S2E15.

administration policy, and what he perceives as his daughter sticking her nose into politics where it doesn't belong. Dealing with the former problem, Josh Lyman pays Griffith a visit and asks her to resign. She refuses; if the president wants her gone, he'll have to fire her.

After the jaw-dropping behavior of the Bush Administration, the pro-science openness of the Obama years was all too welcome.

"The good news is that President Barack Obama's administration, with a Nobel laureate as secretary of energy, a restored White House science adviser, and many other distinguished researchers in positions of major influence, represents a dramatic step forward for science and its role in public life," wrote Chris Mooney in 2009,[84] the year Obama took office. "The 'reality-based community' has been reinstated in Washington; after the Bush administration and its 'war on science,' it feels like a sunrise. Yet we can't expect the long-standing gap between scientists and the broader American public to disappear overnight, meaning this is no time for satisfaction or complacency. If the metaphorical 'war' on science is over, now's the time for the long and difficult process of 'nation building' - for laying sounder foundations to ensure it doesn't come raging back." (Little did he know!)

The Obama Administration was terrific on accurately framing climate issues with scientific integrity. Creating and implementing a Climate Change Action Plan[85] in coordination with the 2015 Paris Agreement that united more than 200 countries in a commitment to address climate change, it was the culmination of years of effort not only to focus the nation's considerable federal resources on the problem, but to engage the cooperation of mayors, governors, and businesses in the mission. It followed Obama's participation in the Copenhagen Accord (2009) and his administration's 2014

---

[84] In *Unscientific America: How Scientific Illiteracy Threatens Our Future.*

[85] See https://obamawhitehouse.archives.gov / president-obama-climate-action-plan.

partnership with China in committing to reducing greenhouse gas emissions long-term.[86]

Obama's science advisor, John Holdren, was a climate change firebrand, in contrast to Marburger. A MacArthur Fellow with a Stanford doctorate in aerospace engineering and theoretical plasma physics, he came to the White House post with a bulging portfolio, having published on climate change policy in *Scientific American*[87] and with the Brookings Institute. He had previously served as a science advisor to Bill Clinton, and took over as Director of the Office of Science and Technology Policy in March 2009 by a unanimous vote of the Senate.

He could not have been a more overt contrast to Marburger. His message on climate change (and many other policy areas with essential scientific dependencies) reached beyond the media into the Obama Administration's effort to coordinate federal efforts with research and engineering initiatives around the world. More than an ambassador for science, he was a diplomatic troubleshooter, smoothing the path for alliances with other governments and private industry. Obama got the credit; it was Holdren who moved the mountains.[88]

And then there were the pandemics - the eruption of Ebola in West Africa in 2014, which threatened the US when a man in Dallas, having traveled to the US from Africa, was found to have the virus. He died. Ten additional cases emerged; all but one recovered.

Ebola was more scare than reality in the US, but that didn't stop Holdren; he went on PBS, describing high-tech measures to treat while containing; he met with private-sector scientists, preparing for

---

[86] *The West Wing*, of course, tackled fuel emission standards in "The Stackhouse Filibuster" (S2E17), when John Hoynes – a Texan fossil fuel industry advocate, despite being a Democrat – suddenly flips and takes the side of the angels, pushing back against industry protests over the Bartlet Administration's initiative on fuel additives.

[87] In *The Future of Climate Change Policy: The US's Last Chance to Lead.* Scientific American 2008 Earth 3.0 Supplement. October 13, 2008, 20–21.

[88] During the Obama Administration, the president and his science advisor and their team managed to bring domestic carbon emissions down 9 percent, while growing the economy more than 10 percent.

the worst; and he led a task force created by executive order to combat antibiotic-resistant bacteria.

Five years earlier, a new virus – H1N1 – had appeared in the US, prompting Obama to declare a national emergency. More than 12,000 Americans died of the virus, but federal response was swift and effective; a vaccine was successfully deployed, and the crisis was ended by April 2010. Holdren's role? To lead an effort to overall the vaccine distribution process to get to more people more quickly, an effort he openly presented to the media, to reassure the public.

Ah, the good old days...

Anthony Fauci in the Hot Seat

We have, then, two extremes: the expert voice in the White House that tells it straight and won't back down, and the expert voice that dissembles and prevaricates for political gain.

But back in the Bartlet West Wing, it's the expert telling it straight and the administration itself dissembling and prevaricating for political gain. In the end, however, Bartlet doesn't disappoint. Griffith does offer her resignation, and they summarize the problem:

"On thinking about it, I felt your firing me would send a dangerous signal to whomever had my job next," she explains.

"Did you not think that playing down the dangers of drug use sent a dangerous signal as well?" he asks.

"I do not believe that is what I did, sir," she replies, and of course she's correct; she's grounding the debate back in the reality of the words actually spoken, defusing the political trimmings: "I was asked, by and large, if marijuana holds the same addictive properties as heroin or LSD; it does not. I was asked if marijuana poses a greater health risk than nicotine and alcohol, and in my opinion, it does not."

And that brings us to another high-profile healthcare professional speaking truth to power, who in 2020 was faced with Griffith's dilemma: Dr. Anthony Fauci, Director of the National Institute of

Allergy and Infectious Diseases, an honest and effective scientist and administrator who served six administrations, having taken his post in 1984.

At age 79, Fauci faced the challenge of a lifetime for a professional of his particular specialty: the coronavirus and the global eruption of the COVID-19 pandemic. That it happened while Fauci was the top-ranking epidemiologist in the US was certainly fortunate; that it happened on Donald Trump's watch most certainly wasn't. Fauci could not have been more equal to the task; Trump couldn't have been less so.

Fauci, who had been at Barack Obama's side through several pandemics had, in fact, predicted the coronavirus or something like it on the Trump watch: in January 2017, during an address to the Center for Global Health Science and Security at the Georgetown University Medical Center – 10 days before Trump's inauguration – he said the following:

"If there's one message that I want to leave with you today, based on my experience... there is no question that there will be a challenge to the coming administration in the arena of infectious diseases - both chronic infectious diseases, in the sense of already-ongoing disease, and we have certainly a large burden of that, but also there will be a surprise outbreak... History, and the history of the past 32 years that I've been the director of NIAID, will tell the next administration that there's no doubt in anyone's mind that they will be faced with the challenges that their predecessors were faced with." The title of the panel: "Pandemic Preparedness in the Next Administration."

And when Fauci's prediction came true in January 2020, it was he who stepped to the presidential podium to begin informing the public about the coronavirus; it was he who explained what it was and what it meant; it was he who outlined the steps necessary to limit the spread of the virus; it was he who offered up reasonable, fact-based predictions about what would happen next.

His narrative didn't come close to matching Trump's. In the early weeks of the pandemic, he careened wildly from one fictional statement to another: the virus was a hoax; the virus was a Democratic scheme to thwart his re-election; the virus was a vengeful Chinese attack on the US.

When the existence of the virus could no longer be denied and Americans were dying, his rhetoric shifted, but its unstable dynamic remained: the virus would just magically disappear before summer; it could be cleared up by injections of disinfectant; bright light shining inside the body would do the trick; and there's this hydroxychloroquine stuff...

And running parallel to Trump's snake oil pitches were his reports on his administration's success in coping with the pandemic. As the US rocketed to the front of the international pack in cases and deaths, he steadily reassured the public that he was doing an "outstanding" job of containing COVID, repeatedly insisting that if there was less testing, there would be fewer cases.

A disconnect of this magnitude between President and Expert was unprecedented. Fauci and Trump could not have offered more radically disparate accounts of the nation's reality.

It went far beyond Leo censoring the EPA, or Josh prioritizing a White House official position over medical truth, or CJ speaking for herself and not the White House; those exemplars of executive disconnect pale beside the Fauci-Trump collision. But they are connected, and in-kind, on a deeper level: they all speak to the confusion such disagreement generates in the public, on the question of who to trust. And when the coronavirus came to town, that trust was already all over the map, in the mind of the American public. As of Summer 2020, Newsweek was reporting that "a majority of Republicans say they don't trust Dr. Anthony Fauci or the Centers for Disease Control and Prevention (CDC) for advice on the coronavirus, but almost 70 percent say they trust President Donald Trump for advice... 52 percent of Republicans said they don't trust what the CDC has said about the novel virus, and 53 percent said they don't trust Fauci," according to a poll it took.

By contrast, *Newsweek*'s poll revealed that among Democrats, "a large majority said they don't trust Trump for advice on the virus but do trust Fauci and the CDC. According to the poll, 93 percent of Democrats said they don't trust the president, while 78 percent said they trust Fauci and 76 percent said they trust the CDC."

With partisan affiliation removed from the data, the results indicated that "among all respondents, 31 percent said they trust Trump for advice on the virus, 51 percent said they trust Fauci, and

55 percent said they trust the CDC. By comparison, 58 percent said they don't trust what Trump has said about the virus, 29 percent said they don't trust Fauci, and 32 percent said they don't trust the CDC."

That kind of divide is unconscionable, certainly; but the numbers lay out in stark, disheartening transparency just how messed up the collective mind of the American citizen has become, when it comes to trusting experts – and more alarming, how off-the-charts its misplaced devotion to an authoritarian leader can be.

Per Fauci, the US is "still knee-deep in the first wave" of the pandemic; per Trump, "I think we are in a good place."

Fauci dared not openly criticize the president, lest he be dismissed (and he sorely needed to remain where he was, for the good of the nation). Trump, predictably, had no compunctions about criticizing Fauci, speaking openly to the media about the NIAID director's "mistakes."

And even that wasn't the worst of it; for daring to continue putting data ahead of authoritarian bloviation, Fauci revealed in early August that he and his family had been getting death threats, and that he had been forced to arrange private security to protect them.

"I wouldn't have imagined in my wildest dreams that people who object to things that are pure public health principles are so set against it and don't like what you and I say, namely in the world of science, that they actually threaten you," he said.

That's how far we've wandered from the truth.

"A sluggish response by a government denuded of expertise allowed the coronavirus to gain a foothold," summarized Ed Yong in *The Atlantic*. "Chronic underfunding of public health neutered the nation's ability to prevent the pathogen's spread. A bloated, inefficient health-care system left hospitals ill-prepared for the ensuing wave of sickness. Racist policies that have endured since the days of colonization and slavery left Indigenous and Black Americans especially vulnerable to COVID-19. The decades-long process of shredding the nation's social safety net forced millions of essential workers in low-paying jobs to risk their life for their livelihood. The same social media platforms that sowed partisanship and misinformation during the 2014 Ebola outbreak in Africa and the 2016 US election became vectors for conspiracy theories during the 2020 pandemic."

"Openness is the Basis of a Free Society"

Sometimes President Bartlet got it right, of course, as when a fire in a national forest sparks controversy over the federal government's responsibility to fight it.[89] Public sensibility (and an anxious governor) favor the federal government putting the fire out; but his environmental science advisers tell him not to:

"It's the end of the season and the fire isn't anywhere near tourists," he tells Leo." Letting this fire burn is good for the environment. You know how I know?"

"How?"

"Because smart people told me. Please, god, Leo, let them be right..."

And Sam weighs in on professional expertise, peaking not only for progressive politicians everywhere but the majority of the electorate. He's arguing with film producer Morgan Ross about the impact of TV violence on children.[90]

"There's been a 28% drop in juvenile crime in the last five years, 10% drop in the overall crime rate," Ross tells Sam.

"I don't care," Sam replies.

"Why?"

"Because the American Academy of Pediatrics, the AMA and the American Psychological Association all say that watching violence on TV is bad for kids," Sam explains, "and we're gonna listen to the experts..."

But the last word on this subject will go to Ellie, who found herself mired in White House controversy once again in "Eppur Si Muove",[91] when a partisan attack on Bartlet was opportunistically

---

[89] In "Ways and Means", S3E3.

[90] In "Ellie".

[91] S5E16.

based on her working as a research assistant for a controversial cervical cancer study that included sex workers as subjects. Bartlet is less harsh with his daughter this time around, as she obviously just wants to be left alone to do her work, but her father convinces her that science can't extricate itself from public controversy - there are times when she and those like her must take a stand.

This she does, behind the briefing room podium, giving this statement:

"While money spent studying the brains of PCP users might seem to be taxpayer waste, this research led directly to the discovery of the NMDA receptor. Science cannot exist in a vacuum. By nature, it's an open enterprise, strengthened by public scrutiny. Openness is the basis of a free society. But when science is attacked on ideological grounds, its integrity and usefulness are threatened. Independent peer-reviewed research is the cornerstone of science in America. It shouldn't be about the left or the right, but what works to keep people safe and healthy. I believe all Americans, and all people everywhere, no matter who they are or how they live, deserve research to improve their lives. Thomas Jefferson said, 'We must not be afraid to follow the truth, wherever it may lead.' Scientific truth ennobles us. It tells us who we are, where we've been, and where we're going. I believe the truth will only be found when all scientists are free to pursue it."

Duty! Sublime and Mighty Name

Presidential Competence

Sam Seaborn and Associate White House Counsel Ainsley Hayes, the Bartlet Administration's token Republican, are in Toby's office, doing what they do best: arguing...[92]

"Does it concern you," Ainsley asks Sam, "that the smartest Presidents have been the worst?

"I don't grant your premise!" he replies.

"John Quincy Adams was so full of himself he could hardly build a coalition around having eggs for breakfast," she continues. "And how many grand theories of international relations did Wilson come up with that were dead on arrival in Congress?"

"I don't care," Sam declares.

"Why?"

"Because before I look for anything, I look for a mind at work," Sam argues. "Nobody's saying the president needs to have a tenured chair in semiotics, but you have to have-"

"What?"

"-*gravitas*."

"And how do you measure that?"

"You don't," Sam admits, "but we know it when we see it..."

This exchange passively reveals Sam's admiration of President Bartlet, but Sam admires Bartlet for good reason; and it brings into focus another aspect of the Bartlet White House: its overwhelming competence, and that of its central figure in particular – the president himself.

This is an especially valid theme at this writing in 2020, when the United States – struggling to survive a once-in-a-century pandemic and a tanked economy, as well as coping with surging racial unrest –

---

[92] In "The US Poet Laureate", S3E16.

has spent four long, tiring years suffering staggering incompetence. The administration of President Donald Trump has been an unprecedented parade of it, from his ill-conceived executive orders on immigration to his incessant mismanagement of the nation's trade relationships, from his exacerbation of racial unrest to his bungling of the national response to the coronavirus. There has never been such a surge in White House ineptitude in living memory.

We would do well at this moment in our national story to ponder both the necessity of presidential competence and the consequence of its absence. We are informed in that pondering by *The West Wing* – and our own experiences with US presidents over the past couple of generations.

President Bartlet's Republican challenger in the re-election campaign, Florida Governor Rob Ritchie, isn't the sharpest knife in the drawer. Incurious, not particularly knowledgeable, Ritchie is described by Bartlet as having "turned being un-engaged into a Zen-like state."

While roaming Southern Indiana, Josh and Toby take stock of Ritchie: he says "frivolous law firms" when he means "frivolous lawsuits"; he thinks that Sarajevo and Bosnia are two different countries; that Mexico is part of NATO; and, finally, "a rising tide sinks all boats."[93]

Josh gets even more captious; so detached and absent is Ritchie that Josh considers him an unfit opponent, and upon discovering that the Republican candidate has taken counsel from a pop self-help guru, tasks Donna with doing undercover research to explore its vacuity, sending her to one of the guru's seminars:[94]

"What did he say?"

"This is cheap... so the guy's counseled for Ritchie. He's a buffoon, but he's harmless. Why should it be part of the campaign?"

"Because it's not harmless in an American President."

---

[93] In "20 Hours in America, Pt. II", S4E2.

[94] In "The US Poet Laureate", S3E16.

"Nothing he said was wrong or objectionable. As supposed to the man who was sitting next to me, whose name was Fern."

Josh hands the self-help guru's book to Donna.

"Open this book to any page." She does, and hands the book back.

"'It's good to be trapped in a corner,' he reads, '"That's when you act.'"

"That happens to be true."

"It is. In my case, it's the only time that I do."

"So?"

"It's Immanuel Kant!" Josh exclaims. "'*Duty! Sublime and mighty name, that embraces nothing charming or insinuating but requires submission.*' Every year a million freshman philosophy students read that sentence."

"And change their major?"

"You've just got a mouthful of wiseass today, don't you?"

"So he cribbed Kant," Donna says, "Isn't that what you're supposed to do?"

"It comes from a 193-page book called *A Critique of Practical Reason*," Josh replies. "It's about metaphysics and epistemology. Tomba's impressively boiled it down to two-thirds of one page. Give me another one."

"'Look outside the cave.'"

"Right. That's from an old paperback called *The Republic*, by Plato. Lucky Tomba's been able to fit it on a fortune cookie so it suits the attention span of the Republican nominee," he says. "Here he quotes Robert Frost: 'Good fences make good neighbors.' Did he talk about that?"

"Yeah."

"What did he say?"

"Basically, that if you stay within your personal space, you'll end up getting along with everyone."

"You had to study modern poetry. Is that what Frost meant?"

"No, he meant that boundaries are what alienate us from each other."

"Why did he say, 'Good fences make good neighbors'?"

"He was being ironic. But I still don't see-"

Josh gets really animated:

"What does this remind you of? 'I believe in hope, not fear.' 'I'm a leader, not a politician.' 'It's time for an American leader.' 'America's earned a change.' *I* before *E* except after *C*! *It's the fortune-cookie candidacy!*"[95]

The example of Rob Ritchie informs our ruminations on the importance, not only of gravitas in our national leader, but intellectual curiosity and engagement in the work of the office and the events that populate a nation's daily experience. Toby's complaints over Ritchie's lack of highbrow gravity speak to the expectation he shares with Josh, and that Sam conveys to Ainsley, that the presidency requires "a mind at work."

Toby gets a chance to make his anti-Ritchie case directly the president, one-on-one, during a chess game in the Oval Office;[96] in the process, he clarifies what any reasonable presidency should truly be about, at its core:

"You're a good father; you don't have to act like it. You're the President, you've don't have to act like it. You're a good man – you don't have to act like it. You're not 'just folks', you're not plain-spoken; do not, do not, do not act like it!

"Make it about engaged, and not; qualified, and not. Make it about a heavyweight. You're a heavyweight."

And Josh ties it up once and for all at the end of his discussion with Donna:

"These are important thinkers, and understanding them can be very useful and it's not ever going to happen at a four-hour seminar. When the President's got an embassy surrounded in Haiti, or a keyhole photograph of a heavy water reactor, or any of the fifty life-and-death matters that walk across his desk every day, I don't know if he's thinking about Immanuel Kant or not. I doubt it, but if he does, I am comforted at least in my certainty that he is doing his best to reach for all of it and not just the McNuggets.

---

[95] In "The Red Mass", S4E4.

[96] In "Hartsfields Landing", S3E14.

"Is it possible we would be willing to require any less of the person sitting in that chair? The low road? I don't think it is."

Appendices

The World Before *The West Wing*:

Neoliberalism

As mentioned earlier, the economic ideology of neoliberalism emerged from the mists of the Second World War and the attempts of fascism to seize control of Europe. The premise was simple – overly so, in fact: *create a global economy, and let it run itself.*

Run itself, and everything else.

The authors of this ideology – Milton Friedman, Friedrich Hayek, and Ludwig von Mises, created it in service of a number of prevailing assumptions at its core, in which they invested absolute belief:

- Adam Smith's "invisible hand" would guide that economy to bring about permanent prosperity;
- Government could do nothing but hinder it;
- Unfettered markets would generate a social order more stable and enduring than any government could achieve;
- Property was the cornerstone of the economy, and its protection and preservation would result in subsequent guidelines for human governance;
- Government's only legitimate function was the protection of property and police activity to mitigate invasion and crime.

On a less abstract level, this group believed that the policies that had brought the US back from the brink of collapse – FDR's New Deal – were the road to ruin, and needed to be wrenched out of US economics and politics, for its own good.

This is True Believer territory, to be sure, but the initial group adopting this ideology had no trouble bringing others on board; throughout the Fifties and Sixties, neoliberalism attracted thousands of adherents in US and European business and politics, and persisted as a behind-the-scenes influence of Movement Conservatism, which culminated in the ascension of Ronald Reagan to the White House in 1981.

Reagan was unabashedly neoliberal, spouting its tracts on live television with regularity: "Government is not the solution to our problem; government *is* the problem," the neoliberal mantra, became Republican conservative gospel.

And since that time, for more than 40 years, neoliberal politicians have been pushing to hollow out the middle class that the New Deal created; to eliminate as much government regulation as possible; to curtail taxation as much as possible; to impose austerity on the population, in service of business; to privatize such government institutions as actually managed to be deemed essential; and to eliminate any social function the government might be providing its citizens, apart from military and police protection.

If you can't see exactly this agenda blinking like a neon sign within the GOP's activities over the past few decades, you've been hiding in a rain forest somewhere.

Hartmann, in his book on this subject, isolates the tenets of neoliberalism that have presented as the Reagan Revolution has reshaped US economics and government:[97]

- Controlling inflation is job #1 in economic regulation, and austerity (keeping the government out of the social support business) is the best way to achieve it.
- Deregulation of national economies is essential because the market is smarter than government.
- Government enterprises like utilities and healthcare and schools should be privatized.
- Governments must be radically reduced in size and stripped of power, so the markets can do their thing and the very wealth can run them.
- Taxes should reduced as far as possible, covering only the military and police.

---

[97] In "The Hidden History of Neoliberalism", 2022.

- No nation should be favored in this scheme; "nations" should become meaningless. The world should be comprised of markets, not nations.
- Property rights trump human rights; and social discrimination and the economic inequality they foster can be solved by the free market and the people who run it, not by government.

Those core tenets, Hartmann wrote, produce many corollaries:

- Markets are superior to votes – capitalism is superior to democracy. Neoliberalism should be imposed, then, whether citizens like it or not.
- It's okay to restrict the free movement of people between nations, but not the free movement of goods and money.
- The government should have no role in the lives of its citizens outside of law enforcement and a defensive military.
- The family is the metaphor for governance, with a strong father figure who dominate the rabble via authority and the establishment of clear gender roles.
- The welfare state must end; it steals from those who work hard and destroys any incentive in those who don't.
- Government certifications, even the qualifying of physicians and airline pilots, etc., represents free-market interference.
- Even fascism and oligarchy can be seen as acceptable alternatives to welfare-state democracy.
- Competition, not cooperation; winners should be celebrated, and losers ignored.
- Inequality is a sign that society is working as it should; the market rewards the most competent and abandons the least.
- The citizens of a country should be viewed as consumers, first and foremost, because that is their role in the economy and the economy is the true engine of society.
- Monopolies are acceptable because they are signs of great efficiency.

- Labor unions are an impediment to the economy.
- Controlling inflation trumps preventing unemployment.
- Tax havens for the wealthy corporations are an economic and social good, because they reward hard work and innovation and starve the government beast.

The difficulty with this entire ideology, as with most ideologies, is in its foundational assumptions:

- The infallibility of Adam Smith's "invisible hand"; that market activity is the most effective engine of human activity, capable of generating order in all human affairs, from the economy to government to family life;
- Democracy is inherently dangerous, unstable, untrustworthy, inconsistent, and to be constrained, lest individuals band together to corrupt the operation of the market;
- Law and order should be market functions, not government functions; there exists among human beings a natural moral sensibility – it is wrong to steal and kill, and so forth – and the market can eventually reward good behavior and punish bad behavior far more effectively than governments.

It's hard to know where to start, isn't it? The neoliberal take on human nature is probably the right place, with its very incorrect assumptions about how Adam Smith himself perceived human nature (neolibs love to quote *The Wealth of Nations* but seldom bother with *The Theory of Moral Sentiments*). The core belief is that human beings are naturally selfish and focused on gaining advantage, but in fact, most are not; social psychologists have long noted that in the youngest of children, the desire to help emerges early. Most people don't focus on their self-interest, and are in fact not particularly adept at acting in it; to suppose that the "invisible hand" of self-interest is guiding anything at all is a complete abstraction not grounded in evidence.

As for democracy corrupting the marketplace, we've had decades now to study the corruption of the marketplace, from the gobblingup of savings & loans after the suspension of Glass-Steagall to the breathtaking 2007 meltdown of the real estate market in the wake of mortgage-backed securities. When neoliberal business has the opportunity to cheat, steal, or take advantage, it pounces; it has no need of "democracy" to step in to provide a corrupting influence.

And the lawlessness that followed, for which we all had front-row seats, says all that needs saying about the natural "moral order" that neoliberals seem to assume is in place. No, the market doesn't punish wrongdoing at all; it encourages it. It does not hold those who manipulate it and use it for exploitation in any way accountable; it celebrates their success in doing so.

There's much more to learn and much more to say about neoliberalism and its staggering impact on US politics and economics over the past two generations. The reader is encouraged to dive in and study the subject earnestly. Much of the current landscape becomes very clear in that context.

The World After *The West Wing*:

Authoritarianism

Since *The West Wing* first aired, the world has seen a sharp rise in Authoritarianism – the anti-democratic enforcement of the will of an individual or dominant minority at the expense of everyone else's personal freedom. It already ruled in China and Russia; it has arisen in Europe and, through Donald Trump, his MAGA hoards, and those extreme right-wing radicals sharing their fringe, here at home.

Robert Altemeyer, the congenial Canadian psychologist who has led the world's research on Authoritarianism, sought to understand social aggression – the systematic heaping of hostility of one group onto another, a defining feature of our world.

Following up on physicist Steven Weinberg's famous quote about "getting good people to do evil things – that takes religion," he took his research into the behaviors of the Authoritarian Follower a few extra steps, asking the question, What makes otherwise calm and peaceful people aggressive against others?

It turns out to be a complex mix, and it took him many years.

Working from his already-tested Authoritarian scale, he surveyed hundreds of high-Authoritarian subjects, and here's what he discovered:

Fear is the first essential ingredient in Authoritarian aggression. For an Authoritarian Follower to be moved to group violence against another group, they need to be fearful of those against whom they're aggressing.

This makes complete sense, because that's the evolutionary purpose of fear.

But fear alone is clearly not enough; many if not most fearful people choose flight over fight – they simply avoid those who make them frightened or uncomfortable.

Altemeyer found the next piece – *Anger*. The difference, in the animal kingdom (and even more so in the world of humans) between the fearful who fight and the fearful who flee is anger. Fear centers attention on the object of our terror, and where anger is absent, we run; where anger is present, we aggress.

Even so, there are plenty of people who are afraid of others and feel constant, smoldering anger and resentment of those who are making us uncomfortable, yet never rise up against them. Altemeyer had not yet completed the equation.

Aggression is a social act, especially when one group rises up against another group. That remaining missing piece, he found, was a social trigger: moral superiority.

The social response of the Authoritarian Follower to those others who make them afraid and angry is to diminish their humanity, and in so doing, enhance their own. Self-righteousness – I am better than you! – achieves both: *I am better... more worthy... more entitled!* And in a group: *We are better... we are more worthy... we are more entitled!*

And now we have ourselves an Authoritarian ballgame. Brown shirts. A klan.

Our problem is this: the core triggers of aggression – fear and anger – are perfectly natural, and exist in *all* of us, to some degree. They've been with us for millions of years, and they're not going away anytime soon.

But thanks to Bob Altemeyer, we can now be pretty certain that *social* aggression hinges on that last component –self-righteousness. Without it, aggression is a smoldering ember, rather than a forest fire.

And that's something we *can* do something about. The nature of social groups, how they form and bond and behave, is increasingly well-understood, and a consequence of the value systems we've deployed in the world. How people feel about themselves – and how groups feel about other groups – follows from our social disbursements. If we want to disable and dispel moral superiority, we need to redefine what those words mean, and permeate the world with new and better examples. Hard to do, in such a frightened world – but not impossible. We lack only the will to make it happen.

The Global Change Game

Altemeyer offers us more deep insights into Authoritarianism by way of some experiments he conducted with a team in 1994. They involved the Global Change Game, a simulation of international-level interactions between groups of students, meant to explore issues affecting the planet and humankind as a whole.

The game is played on a world map the size of a basketball court. A group of 70 students or so play the game together, each assigned to one of 10 regions of the world, representing 100 million people. Assets are distributed among the regions, and each has its own set of issues to deal with: health, hunger, deforestation, climate change, energy shortages, encroaching desert, economic instability, international trade, inequality – all of these and more can appear on the horizon of any world region.

Three of the regions are nuclear superpowers. Conventional military power is distributed as it is in the real world, and several start off the game with indigenous poverty – again, as in the real world. Facilitators (faculty members) present each region with problems, and it is left to the teams in each region to reach out to request or offer aid, to enter into alliances, to band together to solve problems or oppose one another and create new ones.

Several of the students declare themselves "Elites" – leaders – and the game allows for such players to squirrel away some of their region's wealth for themselves.

Regions can enter into trade agreements, take in refugees, pollute the oceans, offer humanitarian aid, screw up the world economy, and even declare nuclear war (which ends the game by default). After 40 simulated years of international activity, the game is declared over, and points are tallied to determine the winning region.

The Low-Authoritarians. Altemeyer's innovation was to populate one night's run of the game purely with students who had scored low on his Right-Wing Authoritarian scale – students low in Authoritarianism (the students were not made aware that their RWA scores had anything to do with the game). These students managed to achieve world peace and international cooperation. The 10 Elites (seven men, three women) joined together on Tasmania whenever a crisis arose and solved the problem together.

The three nuclear superpowers chose to disarm, and no war broke out during the playing of the game. An ozone depletion crisis announced by the facilitators was solved with the combined economic support of the wealthiest nations and advanced technology. There were several hundred million deaths resulting from disease and starvation in poverty-stricken countries (Europe sent aid – North America refused). World population at the end of the game was 8.7 billion, but resources were distributed worldwide in such a way as to support almost all of them. Overall, Altemeyer considered it a great success.

The High-Authoritarians. The following night, the game was repeated – this time with students who had all scored *high* on the Authoritarian scale. The Elites (all male) declined to disarm, and instead began heavy militarization. The Middle East region immediately doubled oil prices. The Soviet Union prepared to invade North America. A nuclear exchange followed soon after, ending the game.

The facilitators turned off the lights and described the effects of nuclear winter to the students before restarting the game. This time, the Soviet Union invaded China, killing 400 million. The Elite from the Middle East called a United Nations meeting, but nothing came of it.

The ozone depletion crisis occurred, but no cooperative activity was attempted. The European region made some independent efforts to reduce emissions, but the problem got steadily worse. Poverty and population growth went unchecked around the world. Rather than address their nation's economic challenges, the Elites maneuvered for personal power. Alliances

were formed, with stronger partners forcing weaker ones to buy in.

At the end of 40 simulated years, the planet was coming apart, facing mounting crises, armed to the teeth and ready for holocaust. A total of 1,700 million people were dead. The Elites had plundered their regions for personal wealth.

And these were college students!

"There they were, in a big room full of people *just like themselves*, and they all turned their backs on each other and paid attention only to their own group," Altemeyer wrote later. "They too were all reading from the same page, but writ large on their page was, 'Care About Your Own; We Are *Not* All In This Together'."

The implications of these experiments are staggering. These two groups of students varied *only* in their test scores on the RWA Scale; in every other way, they were typical college students, ages 18-22, predominantly white, middle-class, with age-appropriate concerns.

Yet when faced with the opportunity to cooperate or enter into conflict, their differing levels of Authoritarianism caused them to behave entirely differently.

Think about that for a moment. If that can happen in two evenings of game play among young people who have nothing at stake, it is no surprise to see what we see in the world around us today and throughout history, when power is placed in the hands of adults with these same tendencies and impulses.

The point is this: Since *The West Wing* left the air, we've seen a sharp rise in authoritarianism through the Western world – built on conditions the show itself articulated clearly and repeatedly. It has seen its most prominent exemplar in the behavior of Donald Trump and his MAGA followers, but its prevalence greatly exceeds them.

The next few years will be interesting, to be sure, as this rising authoritarianism crescendoes. As of this writing in late 2023, the tide seems to be turning, as the rule of law reasserts itself and consequences loom for Trump and MAGA.

But one of the lessons of *The West Wing* is patience: "the slow boring of hard boards," as President Bartlet said. A dispensation of justice for Jan. 6 may be forthcoming, but there will be much rebuilding after that. Patience...

WestWingWorld!

Welcome to WestWingWorld, the ultimate Delos adult theme park!

This unprecedented blending of state-of-the-art artificial intelligence, engineering, and dramatic innovation has created an astonishing world-within-a-world, a place where the discerning vacationer may be lost in a reverie of intellectual and philosophical extravagance, intimately celebrating the Washington of Aaron Sorkin in the company of hundreds of androids - "hosts", they are called – so life-like as to be indistinguishable from the other guests!

How does that sound? Who wouldn't want to be part of the Bartlet White House, if only for a few days – battling an opposition Congress, girded in social righteousness, surrounded by colleagues like Chief of Staff Leo McGarry, Deputy Chief Josh Lyman, Communications Director Toby Zieglar, Press Secretary CJ Cregg, and Domestic Policy Advisor Sam Seaborn?

...to say nothing of the man himself, Jed Bartlet, First Lady Abbey Bartlet, the First Daughters, body man Charlie Young, Mrs. Landingham, and the endless cast of supporting players that follow?

Who wouldn't want to relive, up close, the Mendoza Appointment? The Haffley Shutdown? The Santos Campaign? Who wouldn't want to be in the Oval Office for the Death Tax Elimination Act Veto, or Speaker Walken's swearing-in? In the Situation Room for Operation Swift Fury? In the Senate Chamber for the Stackhouse Filibuster? In the National Cathedral for Bartlet's rant against the Almighty after Mrs. Landingham's funeral?

WestWingWorld offers all of this and more! The characters of *The West Wing* come to life in full-scale replicas of the White House, the Mall, Capitol Hill and select sections of Georgetown. More than 140 narratives are available; for those who know all the words of every episode, it's possible to step into the role of any major character, including the president – or you can participate improvisationally as an extra, adding your own accents to Sorkin's beloved stories.

Have you ever dreamed of being Presidents Carter, Clinton and JFK all rolled into one? Then be Josiah Barlet, Nobel Prize-winning ex-governor of New Hampshire, the shortest president since Truman – brilliant, yet accessible; erudite, yet folksy – and try out that Oval Office chair! Get Roberto Mendoza confirmed to the Supreme Court! Holler for Mrs. Landingham! Refuse Toby's resignations! Broker peace between Israel and Palestine! Fail to disclose your multiple sclerosis! All in a day's work.

Or be the president's best friend, the ultra-competent Leo: run the country, inspire your staff, urge the president to roll up his sleeves! Yank the vice president's chain! Endure public humiliation over your past substance abuse; dance with women six inches taller than you; square off against Lord John Marbury; admonish the Religious Right! Get taken out for a walk by a Congressional committee! Relive your heart attack at Camp David!

Are you dour, joyless, self-righteous, and even smarter than the president himself? Then you'll enjoy being Toby Zieglar, identifying Walter Hufnagle's overcoat on the Mall; refusing pie from ex-wife Andy by the Potomac, or providing her with sperm for in vitro fertilization; getting up in the president's face, oh, just about any time; or leaking the existence of a classified military space shuttle to Greg Brock of the *New York Times*. Or just save social security!

What woman wouldn't love to be CJ Gregg for a while? Be the press secretary presidents dream of! Be wittier and quicker on your feet than the entire White House press corps combined; tease Danny Concannon; be stunning in off-the-rack dresses; be *really great* in bed! Then step into the role of Chief of Staff, under the worst of circumstances, leapfrogging all of your male colleagues, without missing a beat!

If you're too arrogant to live and too sexy for your shirt, you'll do well as Josh Lyman – Leo's right hand, supervisor of 1,100 West Wing staffers, and the 101st senator. Bring home the Family Wellness Act; steal the First Lady's $12 million immunization education fund; thwart your activist girlfriend Amy by hiring her boss; take a bullet in the chest and come up swinging! Or work his other side, and diss Mary Marsh on national television; lean on Senator Carrick so hard that he turns Republican; take Donna for granted until she quits and joins the Russell campaign.

And how 'bout that Donna, right? You could *be* her, fighting the good fight alongside Josh every day, building up the know-how and skills that will eventually make *you* a chief of staff yourself, to the next FLOTUS! Live it all, from your brazen on-boarding in the first campaign, to your missile-silo-under-the-Eisenhower-putting-green gaffe, to the Gaza mission and your near-death in the suburban - and your bittersweet moments with Irish photojournalist Colin Ayres.

And if you're cool as all hell but don't need to flaunt it, you'll do well as Charlie Young, the president's body man – smarter than Josh and Sam and CJ put together, loved like a son by the president (don't miss the Paul Revere's Knife Scene!), and loved like a lover by his youngest daughter. You'll wake the president at ungodly hours; watch for symptoms of M.S.; bust Zoey's sexual harassers in a Georgetown bar; have the president himself do your tax return! Proudly refuse immunity in the M.S. cover-up investigation - or experience the existential horror of realizing that it was you, not the president, that the shooters at Roslyn were gunning for.

And, of course, it wouldn't be the West Wing without Sam. You can be the earnest, talented deputy communications director, outshining even the president in your optimism, balancing out that moody Toby with your youthful pluck and constant good spirits. Land the State of the Union! Spar with Ainsley Hayes! Walk out of Gage Whitney on the spur of the moment, just from a glance at Josh's bad poker face; sit with Nancy McNally in the Sit Room, defending Daniel Galt; leak the Ritchie campaign's nasty opposition video by mistake, jeopardizing your boss's re-elect; run for Congress to comfort a hometown widow!

It's not just the characters that make WestWingWorld special; it's the unique experience of living among androids that look and feel and act as real as you yourself.

Are you action-oriented? Do bombs, bullets and mayhem get your engine running? Well, that's no problem, because the hosts of WestWingWorld are just machines – you aren't breaking any laws or truly committing any moral breach! You won't *really* be assassinating Abdul Sharif; you won't *really* be blowing up four high-rated military targets in Syria; when you blow away the shooters in the window at Roslyn, they won't *really* die!

And think of the off-script possibilities: wouldn't it be great to be Secret Service agent Simon Donovan, walk into that convenience store and, instead of being killed, take down both robbers, then do CJ all night long?

Yes, if you've got some mojo that needs indulging, WestWingWorld hosts are *fully functional*, able to cater to the most intimate desires of guests – completely consequence-free, because they're just robots! You can be Sam, and accidentally sleep with a prostitute; be the First Lady, and take the president's temperature "recreationally"; experience a night of shame with the philandering John Hoynes; step out of Charlie Young's shoes, and into First Daughter Zoey's bedroom after hours (or vice versa), right under the president's nose!

Or change *West Wing* history in this domain as well – be Josh, having a campaign fling with Donna on the first campaign, rather than the last; or be Sam, and get it on with Leo's daughter Mallory at the Kennedy Center; be CJ, and decide you no longer have a problem with the press secretary dating a reporter.

Just $40,000 a day is all it takes to bring the imaginary world of Aaron Sorkin's *West Wing* to life – to experience the living, breathing characters we've all loved these many years, to make yourself part of the action! Call or visit our website today, and get started on the greatest, most mentally stimulating vacation of your life!

UPDATE: WestWingWorld will be closing indefinitely, pending extensive review and revision of its revenue model. Due to numerous media revelations of the recent string of guest bankruptcies, foreclosures, exorbitant credit card debt and exhausted retirement accounts, a number of fraud investigations at both federal and state levels have been initiated.

Park administrators have assured the public and press that no malfeasance has occurred, that many guests truly have been spending all that they have, free of coercion or undue influence, to continue being in the park, and have issued the following statement from the Delos public relations office:

"WestWingWorld's inquiry into the recent financial difficulties of its most frequent guests has included extensive exit surveys, compiling their reactions to the narratives in which they have participated. The conclusion of our counselors, as well as outside consultants, is uniform: once guests experience truly good government, immersed in a world of competent, intelligent, committed and principled public servants who forego more comfortable and lucrative lives in order to do some real good – a world where they truly matter, and the greater good ultimately prevails over craven politics and the cynicism of partisanship - they simply cannot bring themselves to ever leave."

If you enjoyed
What's Next? The West Wing Guide to American Democracy,
leave a review on Amazon.com!

See more of
the *What's Next?* series
on the following pages...

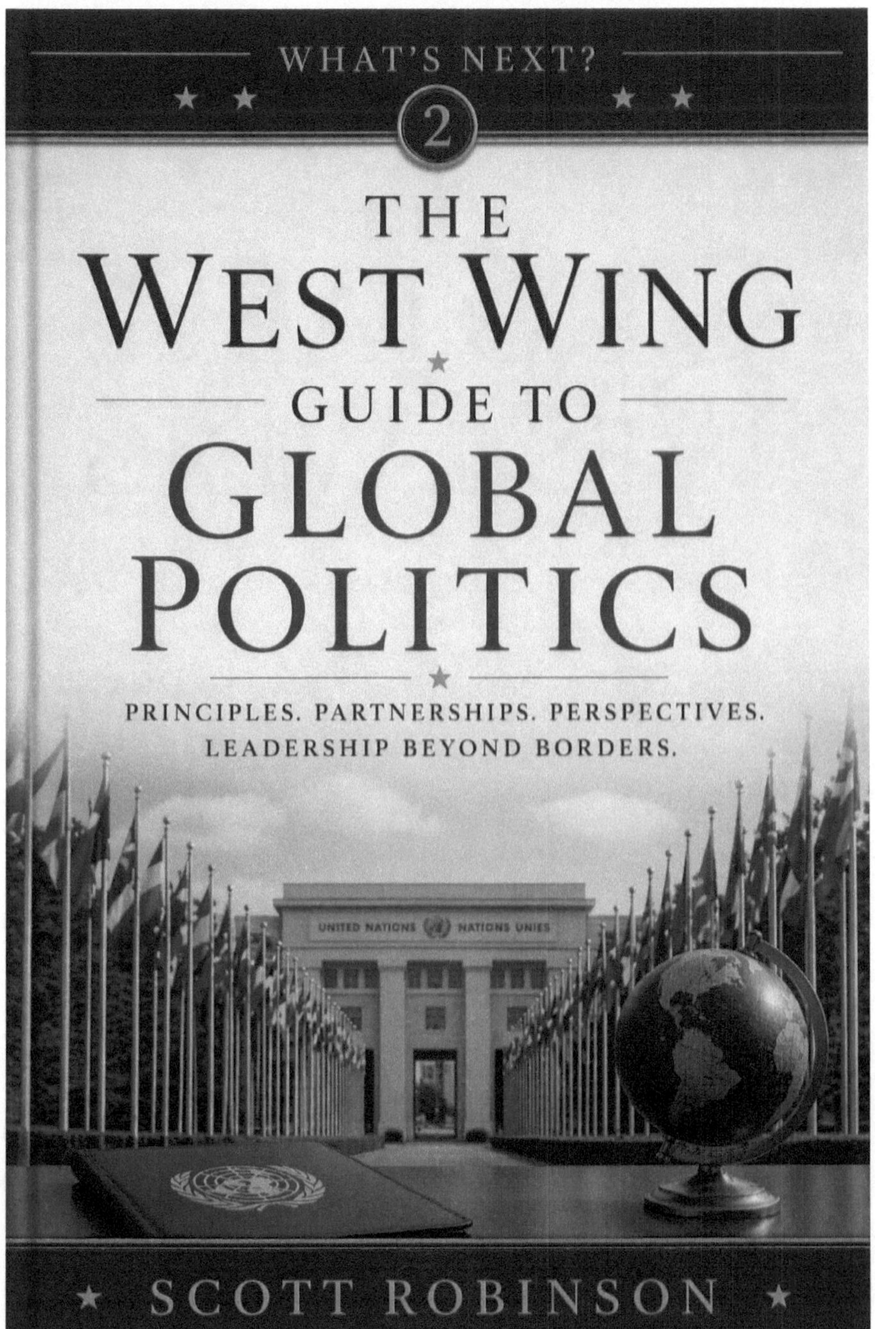
WHAT'S NEXT?
2
THE
WEST WING
GUIDE TO
GLOBAL
POLITICS
PRINCIPLES. PARTNERSHIPS. PERSPECTIVES.
LEADERSHIP BEYOND BORDERS.
UNITED NATIONS · NATIONS UNIES
SCOTT ROBINSON

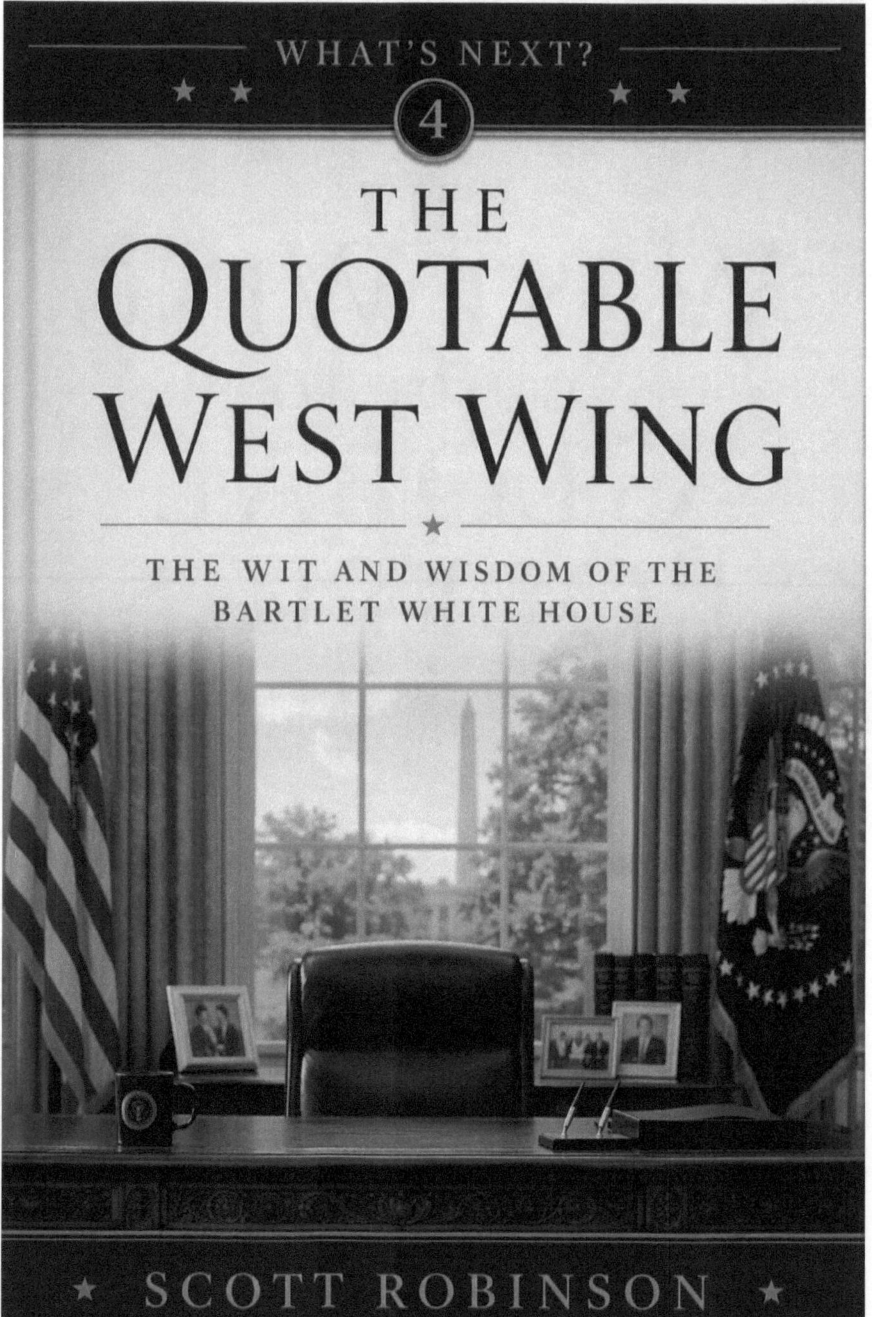
WHAT'S NEXT?
4
THE
QUOTABLE
WEST WING
THE WIT AND WISDOM OF THE
BARTLET WHITE HOUSE
SCOTT ROBINSON

WHAT'S NEXT?
3
THE
WEST WING
ULTIMATE
SUPERFAN
TRIVIA CHALLENGE!
★ TRIVIA QUIZZES FROM ALL 7 SEASONS ★
★ QUESTION: ★
What vegetable does
President Bartlet dislike?
A. Spinach
B. Cabbage
C. Green Beans
D. Corn
THE
WEST WING
★ SCOTT ROBINSON ★

WHAT'S NEXT?
5
THE
WEST WING
BIG BOOK OF
SUPERFAN
FUN!
TRIVIA, STORIES, AND ESSAYS ABOUT
TV'S GREATEST DRAMATIC SERIES!
PRESIDENT
BARTLET
What's Next?
THE
WEST WING
SCOTT ROBINSON

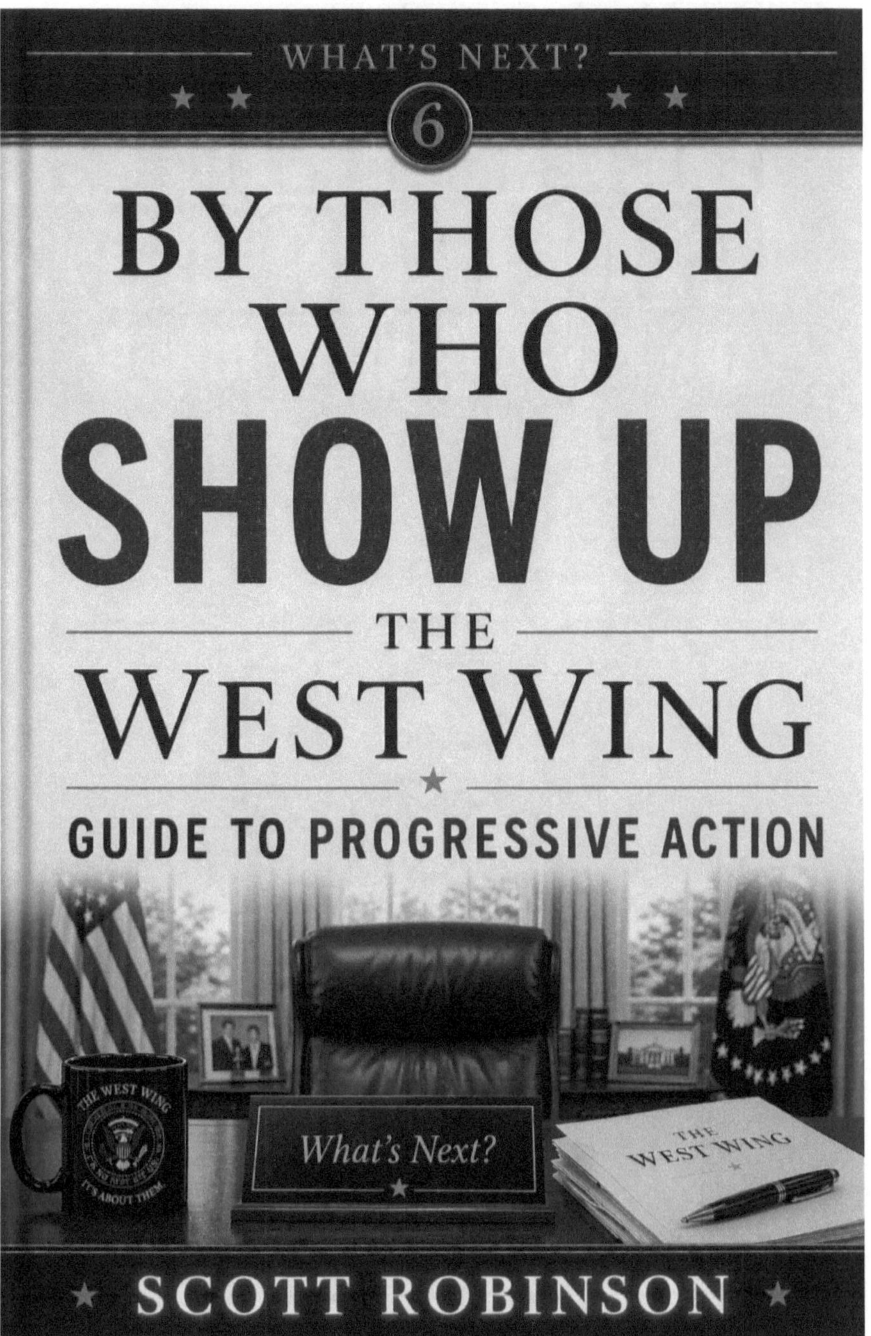
WHAT'S NEXT?
6
BY THOSE WHO WHO SHOW UP
THE
WEST WING
GUIDE TO PROGRESSIVE ACTION
THE WEST WING
IT'S ABOUT THEM
What's Next?
THE WEST WING
SCOTT ROBINSON

RED BRAINS,
BLUE BRAINS
The Psychology of MAGA
Scott Robinson

RED BRAINS, BLUE BRAINS
Authoritarian We Will Go!
Scott Robinson

MILLENNIUM 7
⑦
THEY LONG TO END DEMOCRACY
MINORITY RULE ON THE MARCH
POWER OVER PEOPLE
TRADITION OVER TRUTH
CONTROL OVER FREEDOM
PRIVILEGE OVER EQUALITY
THE THREAT IS NOT LOUD. IT IS ORGANIZED.
SCOTT ROBINSON
⑦

MILLENNIUM 7
7
ZERO-SUM FREEDOM
DEMOCRACY vs. OLIGARCHY IN THE BATTLE FOR LIBERTY
WEALTH DEFENSE
POWER
$
INFLUENCE
CONSUMENT
WE THE PEOPLE
EQUALITY
JUSTICE
FREEDOM
FACTS MATTER
DIGNITY FOR ALL
SECURITY
SECURITY
SECURITY
SECURITY
SECURITY
SECURITY
DEMOCRACY
FREEDOM
EQUALITY
ACCOUNTABILITY
RULE OF LAW
TRUTH
OLIGARCHY
CONCENTRATED WEALTH
CORPORATE CONTROL
POLITICAL CAPTURE
SURVEILLANCE
DIVISION
SCOTT ROBINSON
7

EXPLORING THE ETHICS OF THE FINAL FRONTIER

STAR TREK AND HUMANISM

Living by the Star Trek Ethos in a Troubled World

SCOTT ROBINSON

BOLDLY GOING — BOOK #1

*What would it take to actually build
the world Star Trek imagined?*

PLURIBUS
JOY & DREAD
IN THE BENEVOLENT MACHINE
SCOTT ROBINSON

Sources/Recommended Reading

Books

The Authoritarians, Robert Altemeyer. Cherry Hill Publishing, 2009.

Don't Think of an Elephant! Know Your Values and Frame the Debalte: The Essential Guide for Progressives, George Lakoff. Chelsea Green Publishing, 2014.

The Hidden History of American Healthcare, Thom Hartmann. Berrett-Koehler Publishers, 2021.

The Hidden History of Guns and the Second Amendment, Thom Hartmann. Berrett-Koehler Publishers, 2021.

The Hidden History of Neoliberalism, Thom Hartmann. Berrett-Koehler Publishers, 2022.

The Politics of Millennials: Political Beliefs and Policy Preferences of America's Most Diverse Generation, Stella Rouse and Ashley Ross. University of Michigan Press, 2018.

The Righteous Mind: Why Good People are Divided by Politics and Religion, Jonathan Haidt. Vintage, 2013.

To Make Men Free: A History of the Republican Party, Chris Mooney and Sheril Kirshenbaum, Basic Books, 2009.

Unscientific America: How Scientific Illiteracy Threatens Our Future, Heather Cox Richardson. Basic Books, 2021.

Articles & Papers

Davis, Richard, and Owen, Diana. 1998. *New Media in American Politics*. New York: Oxford University Press.

Florida Communication Journal, Spring 2018, Vol. 46, Issue 1, p91-105.

The Future of Climate Change Policy: The US's Last Chance to Lead Scientific American 2008 Earth 3.0 Supplement. October 13, 2008, 20–21.

Lee McIntyre, "How to Talk to a Science Denier", *Skeptical Inquirer*.

 Owen, Diana. 2017b. "Tipping the balance of power in elections? Voters' engagement in the digital campaign." In *The Internet and the 2016 Presidential Campaign*, Terri Towner and Jody Baumgartner (eds.). New York: Lexington Books, 151–177.

Owen, Diana. 2018. "Trump supporters' use of social media and political engagement." Paper prepared for presentation at the Annual Meeting of the American Political Science Association, August 30–September 2.

Digital sources

FBI Uniform Crime Reporting Program:
https://ucr.fbi.gov/hate-crime/2001/hatecrime01.pdf

https://www.pewresearch.org/shortreads/2017/11/15/assaults-against-muslims-in-u-s-surpass-2001-level/

https://obamawhitehouse.archives.gov/president-obama-climate-action-plan

https://www.bbvaopenmind.com/en/articles/the-past-decade-and-future-of-political-media-the-ascendance-of-social-media

https://www.history.com/topics/women-shistory/womens-history-us-timeline

https://www.pewresearch.org/short-reads/2017/11/15/assaults-against-muslims-in-u-s-surpass-2001-level/

ABOUT THE AUTHOR

Scott Robinson is an artificial intelligence designer, social scientist, public speaker and musician, and serves as Director of Technology and Content for the non-profit Humanity Prime. He has been published in *Rolling Stone* and *The Wall Street Journal*. He can be found at

scottrobinsonwriter@gmail.com

www.ingramcontent.com/pod-product-compliance
Lightning Source LLC
Chambersburg PA
CBHW051443250726

48655CB00001B/215